The Maladroit

Kara Piazza

Writing Piazza Press

The Maladroit
Copyright © 2016 Kara Piazza
All rights reserved.

This book is a work of fiction. All the characters, names, places,
incidents and dialogue in this novel are either products of the
author's imagination or used fictitiously. Any resemblance to
actual persons, places and events is coincidental.

Writing Piazza Press
thewritingpiazza@gmail.com
Library of Congress Cataloging-in-Publication Data Available

ISBN: 0-9969883-0-0
ISBN–13: 978–09969883-0-8

DEDICATION

This is for all my wonderful friends who met The Maladroit on my blog and encouraged me to publish her story. This is also for all my fellow maladroits out there. We should start a club. Who wants to make the t-shirts? Finally, this is for my fellas. When people ask what drives me to push myself so hard, I always tell them it's because I want you to be as proud of me as I am of you. I do better. To infinity and beyond.

ACKNOWLEDGMENTS

I felt I should acknowledge my Lord Jesus for saving me and loving me, not because it's the trendy thing to do, but because it's true. And I must acknowledge God's infinite wisdom in giving me a mother who was also a nurse. I would not have made it this long without this intelligent design. He has blessed me with the incredible gift of creativity, for which I am forever thankful. Any inspired writing I have written comes from Him, and any poor writing comes because I am a flawed human being. I am the first to claim I am not perfect, but I will claim even more boldly that I am forgiven.

CHAPTER 1
Random Run–In

My first vivid memory, perhaps somewhat ironically, is of a concussion I suffered when I was six years old. There was a small pond behind our house that all the neighbor kids liked to skate on in the winter. We weren't wealthy by any stretch of the imagination, so my ice skates were a few sizes too big. Being the resourceful girl I am, I managed to make due.

It was a sunny afternoon. Looking out over the pond, you could see the puffs of air from the warm-blooded children that were working up a sweat across the frozen water. I don't remember the moment it happened, but my friend told me all about it afterwards... after he stopped laughing hysterically. Apparently, both my legs flew up in front of me, and I landed flat on my back. To his credit, my friend Steve stopped laughing when he realized something was wrong.

The woozy feeling was quite memorable, like I might be revisited by the ghost of the lunch I just ate. The walk back to the house was a precarious trip. Steve was there, keeping me from a repeat performance of my Ice Capades maneuver.

I remember laying on the couch and then floating through the room as it suddenly flooded with an ocean of colors, like orange-tinted waves at sunset.

The sounds from the TV were one moment blaring in my ears and the next moment muffled, as though I had somehow sunk beneath the waves of my concussive sea. I remember sleeping and waking up at the hospital. I remember my stomach waging war on its contents. There were feelings of panic when I heard the doctor say I shouldn't be allowed to sleep for fear I might slip into a coma. I wasn't sure what coma meant, but I knew I didn't want to slip into it.

Sadly, this wasn't my last concussion. It was merely the harbinger for things to come. My life is like those comedies where the main character finds themselves repeatedly in situations that seem beyond belief. The hijinks that ensue are painful for the protagonist of the story, but entertaining for those who have a third-person view.

I always hated those kinds of stories, I now know it's because they hit a little too close to home. For a girl doomed to the life being portrayed in those on–screen entertainments, I didn't need to see the show, I lived it. But for those of you blessed to live free from the perils of being maladroit, feel free to laugh. My hope is that you will be entertained by my story. That is after all, why I have chosen to share it with you.

So what makes my story different from all the other tales of accident-prone mundanes? Well to answer that, we have to start at the beginning.

I was born on a simmering, summer evening in mid-July… Just kidding, we don't have to go back that far.

The beginning of this story happened one overcast morning as I was arriving at work. My arms were full of client files, and my purse was haphazardly slung over my shoulder. I was trying to switch my coffee cup to my other hand so I could fish out the keys to my clinic, when suddenly a man came rushing into my peripheral view.

By the time I saw him it was too late to adjust my course trajectory, and the two of us collided in a shower of papers and hot coffee. Now normally my lack of adroitness causes such incidents, but this time I was mercifully free from blame. So proud I was of this fact that I may have overreacted when finally able to blame someone else.

"Why don't you watch where you're going?!?" I shouted.

"Er, ow, yes, I'm so sorry. It's all my fault," he mumbled.

"You're absolutely right it's all your fault! Look at this mess!"

My papers were scattered everywhere. My cup of coffee had somehow turned into a bucket of coffee and covered nearly every inch of paper nearby.

"Here, let me help you," he said softly. He was bent over, so all I could see was the top of his head.

I ducked my own head to hide the blush creeping to my cheeks as I inexplicably thought of running my fingers through his thick, brown locks. I sighed as I collected my papers, shaking off as much white chocolate mocha as I could. I risked a glance, and our gaze met over a soggy paper we had both reached for. His blue eyes sparkled in the morning sun. His chiseled jaw was so magnificent even Michelangelo's David would be jealous. He seemed familiar to me though I knew I would remember having met such a perfect specimen of the male gender.

The way he looked at me caught me off guard. I wasn't used to such intensity. I tried to hold his gaze, but it was like staring into the sun. I was precariously balanced on my toes, and I felt myself losing the battle against gravity.

"Not again."

It was all my brain could think to have my mouth call out as I toppled forward into Blue Eyes' muscular arms. Once more we both crashed to the ground. I thought the brown-haired man would be angry about being bulldozed to the pavement for the second time in a matter of minutes, but I felt him shake with laughter underneath me. As we untangled ourselves, he finally calmed himself enough to sputter a question. "Not again?" His eyes crinkled at the corners from the stunning smile on his lips.

On cue, my cheeks burned brightly, right up to my ears, and I grimaced. But there was something infectious about his laugh, and I soon found myself gasping for breath between peals of laughter.

When the hilarity finally subsided, he helped me to my feet. He deftly plucked up my keys and handed them to me. I unlocked the front door and then turned back to gather up the remaining papers.

"Are you a veterinarian?" He asked suddenly.

This caught me by surprise, which I demonstrated with a moment of awkward silence punctuated by a blank stare. My mouth fell open and I breathed like a caveman. Then he pointed to the sign over the door I just opened, which announced that this was a veterinary hospital.

I smacked my forehead and croaked out a quick, "Yes."

I crammed as many papers into my arms as possible. I tried to convince myself that I would never see this man again, so I should stop acting like my embarrassment was life threatening. *I don't even know the man's name. Why should I care what he thinks of me?*

"My name's Henry," he announced, as though he could read my thoughts.

"I'm Kaly," I blurted out.

"I've never met a pretty veterinarian before," he said.

He mistook my dumbfounded look for disbelief and quickly added, "It's true!"

I tried unsuccessfully to get my brain to pull it together. The smack to the forehead obviously hadn't done any good because I still couldn't form coherent thoughts.

Henry kept talking though, as if the most mortifying thing hadn't just happened. "Do you enjoy being a vet?" he asked.

I nodded. Looking around, I noticed all the papers had been retrieved. Instead of handing them over, Henry continued to hold onto his armful of papers. I didn't know what else to do, so I turned and walked into the clinic. I thought I heard him follow me in, but I was too much of a chicken to turn around and check.

I dumped my papers on the reception desk. I'd let Jenny sort it out when she got in later. Henry added his stack to my pile but didn't show any signs of leaving.

"Do you have any animals?" It was the first question my desperate brain could think to ask.

He nodded. "I have a bulldog named Mortimer."

He flashed that brilliant smile again, and I felt my brain slide back into its former state of mush.

* * *

Now let's pause here. I know what you're thinking. That this is just some sort of sappy love story. I have to clarify right now, it's not…. At least, that's not what makes my story so special. Any schmoe can fall in love, even a maladroit schmoe such as myself. You'll just have to keep reading to find out what makes my story so unique.

* * *

"Oh, bulldogs are my favorite! Don't tell any of my clients that," I added quickly, letting some of my auburn hair fall down to help hide my face.

He chuckled. "Your secret is safe with me."

"Well, um, thanks for helping me pick up all my papers." I tried to move even farther behind my shoulder length curtain of hair.

"I feel really bad about knocking you down. I'm usually

not so clumsy. Do you have some towels? I could help you clean up a bit."

He was looking around the reception area in a way that didn't quite sit right with me.

"Oh that's okay. My receptionist will be in soon, and she can get it all taken care of. Don't worry about it." I waved my hand dismissively.

"Well at least tell me how you like your coffee, and I'll get you another one."

I paused. Politeness said I should tell him not to bother, but I really needed the caffeine to help me through the day. I had been up late the night before reading a really good book. It was only eight, and I was already dragging.

"If it's not too much trouble?" I said slowly, as I looked up at him.

"Not at all! It's the least I can do. Please, it's no trouble."

I bit my lip and weighed how badly I needed another cup of coffee, and finally I agreed.

"White chocolate mocha... please," I added sheepishly.

"Coming right up! Well, actually, if you don't mind, I'd like to run home and change clothes first. I only live a couple blocks away," he said, motioning to the coffee stains setting into his snug fitting t-shirt.

"Oh, of course. You weren't burned at all were you?" I asked, looking him up and down.

He was a good five inches taller than me, making him about six-foot two. He stuffed his hands in the pockets of his boot-cut jeans that hugged him in the right places.

"What's a couple second-degree burns among friends?"

he said with a lighthearted laugh.

I couldn't help but laugh too.

"Maybe when I come back you can give me a tour of your clinic," he suggested.

I must have made an odd noise because he quickly added, "I've been looking for a vet for Mortimer since I moved here. I'm pretty picky about who I trust to take care of him." He gave me a wink.

"Oh, of course. You could bring him too if you want. We offer daycare for some of our *special* clients. I can get Mortimer a spot if you're interested." I don't know what possessed me to say it.

"Special clients, huh? Being your friend has some great perks I see," he teased.

I suddenly became very busy with some files on the reception desk. I tried to make what I hoped would be a nonchalant sound of agreement, but it came out more like an alien grunting around a mouthful of food.

"Then we'll be back. I'll stop home to change and pick up Mort, and we'll stop on our way back and grab you a coffee. Can you wait that long?" he said with a sly smile that made my heart flutter.

I laughed. "I think I can manage. I'll let Jenny know to expect you in case I'm with a patient when you get back."

He nodded and gave one more look around the room. There was something odd about his inspection. I couldn't put my finger on it, but it wasn't the typical assessment of first-time visitors nor the bored curiosity of long-time clients waiting their turn.

I pushed it out of my mind as I watched Henry swagger out the door and past the front window of my clinic. I was just being paranoid. I blamed it on the mystery thriller I read last night, which got me thinking up crazy conspiracy theories.

I was so busy staring after Henry, I jumped when the bell above the door tinkled again. My receptionist entered the clinic, her eyes as round as half dollars.

"Who was that gorgeous man that just left?!" she breathed. Jenny floated behind the reception desk and tossed her oversized purse into one of the desk drawers.

"A new client," I said, turning abruptly so she wouldn't see the redness of my cheeks.

"He's yummy." Her face didn't match her words. She had just noticed the mess on her desk, and her face was crinkled in disgust.

"Sorry about that. I spilled my coffee." I shrugged.

"Again?" Jenny rolled her eyes.

I didn't answer, I just headed toward the closet-sized space behind one of the exam rooms that I used as an office. My first patient would arrive any minute, and I needed a moment to gather myself. I threw my purse down on my chair and grabbed my lab coat. If I didn't wear it, the clients tended to think I was just one of the interns I had working for me throughout the school year. I closed my eyes and took a couple calming breaths.

"Get it together, Kaly." My self-pep talk needed work.

The intercom buzzed. I took one last deep breath, then went to figure out which exam room Jenny had put my first patient in. The light above room three was lit, so I did a quick knock and entered. I picked up the chart and read through it quickly.

My patient's name was Bubba, and he was brought in because he was having trouble walking. I nearly dropped my clipboard when I finally glanced at my patient. I did a double take when I realized the dog before me was a golden retriever. It was hard to tell since he looked like a furry hippopotamus. The walking difficulties the poor thing was having were due to being morbidly obese. I had never seen such an extreme case in all my seven years at the clinic nor in my four years of veterinary school.

I gave a stern lecture to the owner for letting it get so bad and informed them that they would have to schedule a surgery to remove some of the fat.

"Doggie liposuction?" The man stuttered.

"I didn't know there was such a thing," the woman with him commented.

"Something like that." I raised a shoulder in half a shrug.

I wrote my instructions on the chart and told them to see Jenny to schedule surgery as soon as possible. I knew the strain it put on poor Bubba, and I wanted to help alleviate it quickly. When they left, the intercom gave a different buzz, indicating Jenny wanted to talk now that I wasn't with a client.

"Hey Jenny," I said into the phone attached to the intercom.

"He's back," she whispered.

"What? Who?" My mind drew a blank after the shock of my previous patient.

"Mr. Eye Candy!" She was still whispering.

"Um, okay?"

"He's got his dog with him, and he says he's ready for his 'tour' now." She made the benign word sound completely scandalous.

"Oh, right. Well, I have more patients to see. Can you just show him around, please?"

She sighed angrily into my ear. "I tried to, but he said he'd wait 'til you're available. I don't get it, I mean, he knows what I look like, but he still wants *you* to give him the tour? No offense, of course."

I could practically see her disbelief through the phone. I sighed and rolled my eyes. "I will be right there. Let the next client know I'll be a few minutes," I said.

"Yeah, whatever." Jenny hung up.

I straightened my coat and pulled a few stray dog hairs off my pants before I entered the waiting area. I glanced around the reception desk and caught Henry staring. He jumped to his feet and walked over to me. Mortimer waddled leisurely behind him.

"Hey, here's your coffee, as promised! And this is Mortimer," Henry said, handing me a cup and then waving his newly emptied hand at the bulldog plopped down next to him.

"Thanks. Why don't I take you to our daycare room. If you find it satisfactory, you can drop Mortimer off, and I can give you a quick tour after that," I suggested.

"Sounds good," he said with a shrug of his broad shoulders.

I showed him to the large play area separated from the rest of the clinic by a long hallway. For a few moments we stood watching dogs play from an observation window. It overlooked the open, two-story gym that housed the clinic's doggie daycare. A couple of staff members watched over the dogs as they ran from place to place. Henry gave a small smile and then led Mortimer inside.

Without any prompting, Mort made fast friends with a pug named Neptune, and they were off to explore. With one last look, Henry and I left to tour the rest of the clinic, which took less than ten minutes; my clinic isn't that big. I hated rushing, but I knew my schedule for the day was packed. We ended back where we started, at the door that led out to the reception area.

"Well, that's pretty much it. Did Jenny explain our daycare rates and everything to you?" I asked.

"Yes, she was very… thorough," he said.

I laughed. "Sorry the tour was so quick, but I have other clients waiting. I should really get to it."

"I understand. Thanks for fitting me in. I guess I'll see you when I come back to pick up Mort?" he said hopefully.

"I'm sure I'll be here." I felt my stomach flutter.

He went to leave, but instead of taking the door back to the reception area, he went for the door to my office. He had the door open before I could stop him.

"Oh, that's the wrong way!" I finally managed to say.

He was already a couple steps inside when he realized his mistake. He laughed sheepishly and gave one of his dizzying smiles.

"This definitely isn't the exit. Is this your office? I don't remember this from our tour." His eyebrows raised and my heart changed its rhythm.

"Kind of. Sometimes I do client conferences and make phone calls, but that's about all that happens in there. Not exciting enough to make the tour schedule. It's just a table, phone, and some chairs."

I tried leaning nonchalantly against the shelves of patient files that lined the hallway. I miscalculated my distance and nearly hit my head as I tumbled sideways. I managed to catch myself before falling all the way to the ground but my awkward lurch was painfully obvious.

Henry, bless his soul, pretended not to notice. "Speaking of phone calls. Do you mind if I make one real quick? I think some coffee got on my cell phone. It doesn't seem to be working right now, and I really need to call my office." He pointed a finger at the phone on the table in the middle of the room.

"Of course. Sorry again about the coffee." I willed my cheeks not to turn crimson.

"It was my fault, really. You have nothing to be sorry about. And thanks for letting me use your phone. I promise not to call China or anything," he said with a mischievous grin.

I tried to be witty. "If you did I would just have to add it to your bill."

His laugh was one of the most beautiful things I had ever heard. He had laughed before, but this time he was laughing at a joke I had made.

I was riding high from the experience as I went off in search of my next patient. Henry gave me one last smile as I knocked and entered exam room one. I returned his smile, completely unaware that he would not be coming back to get his beloved bulldog.

CHAPTER 2
Searching for Answers

I sat at my desk and wrote some notes on one of the patient charts from the tidy stack nearby. I hated taking them home with me, so I was trying to finish as quickly as I could before I left for the evening. I glanced down as Mortimer gave a muffled bark in his sleep. He was curled up on the dog bed I had dragged into my office an hour ago. Pick-up for dog daycare had passed two hours ago, and I was starting to grow concerned. I called both the numbers Henry had listed on his paperwork, but there was no answer. I left numerous messages but still had not heard back from Mortimer's master. I reached down and gave Mort a pat.

"Well boy, I don't know what happened to your dad. I hope he's okay."

Yeah, I'm one of those people who talks to animals. A long time ago, I gave up worrying about whether people would think it was weird. I figure as long as they don't start talking back, I'll be okay. Not to mention I have plenty of other things to fill up my "totally embarrassing" mental list.

Like the time I went to camp one summer and kicked off the traumatic bunk bed incident of '99. So many memories are made at camp, but I'm sure, for a select few, this memory will go down in infamy.

⁂

My second night at camp, I was making the long trek back to the cabin from the restroom. It was a clear, starry night. Even though it was the middle of summer, we were up in the mountains, so it was particularly cold. I pulled my jacket tighter around me and shuffled as quickly and quietly as I could towards my bed. I had been assigned the top bunk by someone who knew absolutely nothing about me.

I clamored up onto my bed, looking forward to burrowing deep into my nylon sleeping bag. I hate being cold, so I was in a hurry to be warm once more. I was a bit overzealous with my forward motion as I propelled myself up and onto the bed. The momentum, combined with the sleek surface of my sleeping bag, shot me out like a pinball, bouncing me back and forth between my bunk and the bunk next to mine. I hit my own bed so hard it knocked the wind out of me, and I ricocheted back towards my neighbor's bunk.

I can't imagine what was going through the head of the poor girl I landed on, but the terror in her eyes was evident. She had been awoken from a deep sleep by some large, floundering, wheezing object. I couldn't even explain what was happening to the petrified creature. All I could do was try to suck air back into my empty lungs. It was like trying to suck a grape through a straw.

She screamed, and we thrashed about a while before I finally managed to regain my breath and explain what had happened. The next day she asked for a room change, and I had to see the camp nurse for the bruising that covered most of my back. I had to sleep on my stomach for a week.

It's memories like these that free me up to talk to animals without feeling embarrassed. My bar for humiliation is set rather high.

"How would you like to come home with me tonight?" I asked Mort.

He tilted his head as though he were considering my offer. I stood up and stretched out the muscles that had cramped from a long period of nonuse. I snapped a leash onto the collar around Mort's neck. The collar was crafted from a thick strap of leather. It looked custom made. My concern for Henry grew. Mort was well fed, had an expensive collar, and responded to commands. He was obviously well taken care of. It didn't make sense that his owner would just drop him off and not come back.

I walked out of my office, stopping by the shelves in the storage closet to pick up some bowls and food to take with us. On impulse, I grabbed a couple toys and a dog bed. I knew I should have just put Mort in one of the kennels we used for overnight guests, but I couldn't bring myself to do it. After flipping off the last of the lights, we exited the clinic. Mort waited patiently as I set the alarm and locked the door behind us.

The noises of the city carried on all around us as we walked the ten blocks to my apartment. Sirens and honking horns. Bass thumping from someone's stereo. A steady thrum of traffic. It was a pleasant, warm evening, and we were enjoying one another's company. Mort found many exciting things to smell along the way, and I wasn't in a hurry, so we ambled along at a leisurely pace.

He didn't have any problem with the elevator in my building. He must have ridden them before. He just sat and waited for the doors to open again, not the least bit concerned when the lift began to rise. I let him off his leash once I had my front door latched behind us. He set off, eager to explore his new surroundings. I set up his food and water dishes in my small galley kitchen. I dialed the number for my favorite Chinese food place from memory. I placed an order for sweet and sour chicken and crab rangoon. I didn't even have to give them my name.

Half an hour later, the two of us were settled in like we had been together all our lives. I was ensconced on my large, microfiber couch with Mort curled up next to me snoring away. The leftover Chinese food sat cooling on my glass coffee table. I pulled the crocheted blanket up to my chin and fell asleep to reruns of the Gilmore Girls.

I was awakened by the shrill, incessant ringing of my cell phone. I knocked over some of the food cartons as I searched through bleary eyes for the irritating object. I'm not a morning person, so it's possible I accidentally grabbed the TV remote at first.

"Hello," I growled into what I hoped was my cell phone.

It's not uncommon for my tone in the morning to be construed as hostile, but my caller ignored it.

"Kaly, you need to get over here right away!" The hysterical tone of my receptionist made her sound like a twelve-year-old instead of the twenty-two-year-old I knew her to be.

I sat up quickly, which was a mistake. I hadn't slept in a very comfortable position on the couch. There was a pain in my neck that could put bullet wounds to shame. I tried standing, but one of my legs had fallen asleep and didn't hold my weight. I panicked briefly, still in the fog of sleep, thinking I had somehow lost one of my legs. I was relieved to see them both still attached to my body as I landed next to them on the floor. Mort opened one of his brown eyes to watch the goings-on before he yawned and went back to sleep.

"Kaly? Are you there? What was that crash? Did you fall down again?" Jenny's anxiety now had a twinge of annoyance.

"My leg was asleep. What happened? You know it's my late day." I read the clock nearby. "I don't come in for another two hours," I groaned.

"There's been another break-in," she said.

I sighed and hefted myself back onto the couch. In my years of owning a veterinary clinic in a bustling metropolitan area, I have had my fair share of burglaries. It's always drug seekers. There's only so much you can do to safeguard against it. Locking the drugs up, video surveillance, and an alarm system. It was usually enough to deter even the most desperate ruffians. Most didn't make it past the front door.

"Wait a minute. I didn't get a call from the alarm company." My groggy thoughts were finally coming into focus.

"Did you remember to set it last night before you left?" Jenny asked.

"Of course I set it."

"Cause it doesn't work if you don't set it." She ignored me.

"I know how an alarm works, Jenny." I gritted my teeth.

"When will you be here? You need to get here."

"Did you call the police?" I probed.

"They said it was just someone looking for drugs." Something in Jenny's voice made my heart plummet into my stomach.

"You don't agree?" I asked with growing concern.

"You need to get here," she repeated.

"I'm coming. I just need to get dressed, and I'll be there." I dropped the phone without even ending the call.

I pulled on a pair of my size ten jeans, trying not to think about how I used to fit into a size eight. I didn't even bother fixing my t-shirt when I realized I'd put it on inside-out. It was from some concert I had attended more than a decade ago. It had the faces on it of a boy band I used to love, and I usually only wore it around the house. I didn't give it a second thought as I rushed Mort out the door.

The pounding of my heart only worsened the closer Mort and I got to the clinic. Then for one glorious moment I felt relief when the front of my clinic came into view.

From the outside, it looked like it always did. The landscaping was neatly trimmed. Pictures of happy animals filled the lower half of the large windows on the front of the building. The front door had a few nose prints on the glass.

My relief was shattered the moment I entered my beloved hospital. The place gave a whole new intensity to the word ransacked. The display shelves of dog and cat food were all overturned, every bag sliced open, their contents scattered across the floor. The cushions on the chairs that circled the waiting area were ripped open and stuffing was scattered everywhere. The reception desk looked as though it had expelled every last item from its drawers and cabinets. Even the ceiling tiles were askew. I don't remember when I stopped breathing, but my lungs screamed at me to take a breath before I passed out.

Jenny came rushing out of the door from the back of the clinic.

"What the...." I couldn't even think of the words to finish my sentence.

"The whole place looks like this." Jenny ran a hand through her dishwater blonde hair.

Her blue eyes were wide. They darted back and forth as she once again surveyed the room. They never stayed long on any one thing.

"Did you check on the animals?" I asked, grasping her small hands so she would stop wringing them.

"The animals are fine," she claimed dismissively. "And the daycare area was okay. Then again it's just an open gym full of dog toys, so there wasn't much to disrupt there. I didn't know what else to do, so I let the clients in through the side door like always," Jenny said.

I just stared at her, my mouth hanging open.

"What was I supposed to do?! Toby and Carly said they didn't mind working today. And the clients were counting on dropping their dogs off. I couldn't just turn them away when they showed up could I?" Her voice had risen an octave, and all her words were running together.

"I don't understand what happened here." I couldn't keep the anger out of my voice.

"They weren't looking for drugs, that's for sure." Jenny absently shoved some folders into a drawer.

I frowned. "They didn't take the drugs?"

"No, I mean yes. I mean the drugs are gone. It was the only thing they took." Jenny picked up more papers from the floor near her desk.

I gave a frustrated sigh. Jenny wasn't making sense, but she could get that way when she was flustered.

"You spoke to the police? Did they look at the surveillance tape?"

"They said it's time to update to digital. The tape was wrecked. They said it was from all the times it's been recorded over. The drugs were the only thing missing. They tried to lift some prints from around the drug locker but all they got were smudges. So they wrote it off as a drug theft. But come on, we've seen *that* before and *this*... is something else entirely." She waved her arm to highlight the destruction all around her. "Someone was looking for something, but it wasn't drugs."

Mort gave a whimper. I had forgotten he was even there.

"What else could they possibly be looking for here? We don't have anything else of value besides the drugs. Did they take any of the equipment in the operating room?" I looked around hopelessly.

Jenny shook her head.

I gave a gentle tug on Mort's leash. "I'm going to take him to daycare, and then I'll be back to help clean this mess up."

Jenny was right about the gym. It looked like it always did. Of course, it looked like a pack of wild dogs had been through it before the break-in. The burglars could have been here too, and it wouldn't be noticeable. I dropped Mort off and walked slowly through the rest of the clinic to survey the damage. When I saw the shelves where the client files were kept, I felt like crying. It looked like not a single piece of paper was left where it should be. It would take weeks to get everything back in order.

I tried to run through various scenarios for why someone might have done this, but everything seemed ridiculous or unlikely. Whoever it was, they had been thorough. They'd had plenty of time inside my clinic. They must have come as soon as I left. That thought gave me the jeebies. If they were watching the clinic, then they saw me leave last night. I shuddered and tried to think about something else.

I turned into my cubicle of an office and slid into the

chair behind the desk. I placed my head in my hands and fought back tears. The intercom buzzed, making me jump. I clicked the button and Jenny's voice filled the small room.

"Hey, are you coming back soon? You said you would help straighten up out here."

"Yeah I'll be right there."

With a deep breath, I stood and made my way down the hallway behind the examination rooms, clearing a path as I went. Files were scattered everywhere, and I didn't want footprints all over them.

As I passed exam room two I heard a soft but distinct thud from behind the closed door. I stopped dead in my tracks. The gym and the kennels were on the other side of the building, which meant no one else was nearby except Jenny. After a moment, I chided myself for being so paranoid. Jenny could have entered the room from the other side. There was another set of doors that lead to each of the three exam rooms from the reception area.

"Jenny?" Being the chicken that I am, I called her name without opening the door. "Jenny, is that you?"

There was no answer. I leaned closer to the door to listen. There was silence and then another thump. It was a little louder this time, and I jerked back from the door.

"Jenny? If you're in there tell me! This isn't the time to play around!" I said a little louder.

I took a hesitant step towards the door. What was that thumping noise? Why wasn't she answering me? Was she even in there? If it wasn't Jenny, then who was making that noise? All these questions swirled rapidly through my head.

I tried to turn the doorknob, but my hand was so sweaty that I couldn't get a grip. And I *really* needed to get a grip, literally and figuratively. I wiped my hand on my holey jeans, glad I hadn't worn a nice pair in today. I was already covered in dirt from picking up dusty files in the hall.

My hand trembled as I once again reached for the knob. This time I managed to twist it open. I pushed the door open slowly and peered into the pitch black room. The light from the hallway seemed to be swallowed by some mysterious force, and I was unable to see more than shadows inside the room. I groped along the wall for the light switch. I knew it was somewhere farther ahead, so I took one more step into the room. Suddenly there was another thump, and something large crashed into the back of the door. It slammed shut. My brain went into that zone of fear where you can only focus on one thought no matter how irrational it might be.

All I could think was that I had to find the light switch. I felt desperately along the wall where I knew it was supposed to be. I still hadn't found it when I heard a scraping noise and a low, guttural moan. I stopped to listen, trying to pinpoint where the noise was coming from. The seconds stretched out like hours, but only silence greeted my straining ears.

It felt like someone was toying with me. I was sure they could hear my heart beating from whatever place in the room the coward was hiding. I took a shaky breath and once more frantically started patting my hands along the wall. Silently I prayed to find my only hope of salvation, the small piece of plastic that turned on the lights. Amidst my shuffling steps, I heard the thumping noise again.

This time it was much too close for comfort.

I gave an uncontrolled whimper as I urgently fondled the wall. The thump came again from somewhere near my feet and something sharp grabbed my leg in the darkness. I screamed a bloodcurdling cry of horror, which was answered by some unholy shriek. I kicked out at my attacker as hard as I could. I didn't hit flesh like I expected. Instead I hit something metal that gave off a hollow clang. The sharp pain in my leg was spreading.

Since the instinctual "fight" response wasn't working, my body reverted to "flight" instead. My hip crashed into something as I tried to make my escape. I quickly forgot about the pain in my calf. New agony from my side shot tendrils of liquid fire up and down my body. The jolt sent me spinning then falling. My sense of direction was thrown into utter chaos. As I careened towards the direction gravity demands, my last conscious (but mistaken) thought was that I had found the light switch when brilliant colors suddenly flooded my vision.

Then everything went black once again.

CHAPTER 3

More Questions and Mr. Snuggles

The first thing I noticed was a sharp and burning pain, but I couldn't tell where exactly it was coming from. It grew until it felt as though my whole existence was nothing more than torment. I heard someone calling my name, though it sounded like they were talking through a thick pillow.

I focused on the voice. It was a male voice; familiar, but I couldn't place it yet. The pain started to localize, first to the upper portion of my body, then to my head. I groaned and tried to open my eyes. I was greeted by agonizingly bright lights. Nothing would focus. It was like trying to look through glasses covered in a thick layer of Vaseline.

"Kaly, it looks like you may have a concussion." The familiar voice spoke from the blue-and-white blob that hovered over me.

I rubbed my eyes and blinked a few times. I winced when I lowered my chin to my chest. The pain felt like fire pouring out of a spot on the top of my head. It took a moment to figure out what was happening. Then it all came back to me in a rush – the dark room, the odd noises and… I sat up quickly.

"Someone attacked me!" I shouted.

Then I leaned over to release the contents of my stomach onto the floor. Sitting up so fast was a bad idea.

"Mr. Snuggles," the man said.

I stared at him in bewilderment. He came into sudden focus. I realized the man was Jim, the other veterinarian I had recently hired. As my business had grown, I hired another vet to help with surgeries and appointments. It also gave me the chance to take a break every once in a while.

"I beg your pardon?" I said with no small amount of effort.

Jim scratched his salt-and-pepper beard and gave an embarrassed smile. "It was Mr. Snuggles that attacked you. He managed to get out of his cage and somehow got himself trapped in here."

He waved a hand around to emphasize that "here" meant Exam Room Two where I was now seated, somewhat upright, in the middle of the green, linoleum floor.

"A cat did this to me?!" I screeched, reaching up to gingerly touch the spot on top of my head that radiated pain.

I pulled my hand away and felt a wave of nausea wash over me. Perhaps ironically, there was something about the sight of my own blood that always made me a little woozy. And head wounds bleed profusely. It reminded me of a similar wound I received back in high school.

I went to a small school that only added boys' football to the afterschool activities my senior year. To commemorate this joyous addition, they decided to have a girls' powder-puff game during homecoming week. I was a rather sporty girl (don't scoff, accident-prone doesn't necessarily mean completely uncoordinated, as my stellar work as a veterinarian proves), so I signed up to play for the senior team. We were playing the junior class, and being competitive, I was giving it my all. It was the last play of the game, and the other team had the ball. I watched the snap and the toss, and I took off after the girl who had just barely caught the football. I was faster, and I was gaining on her as we rushed down the field. I had just felt the stiff canvas of the flag in my fingers when the ball carrier slipped past me.

Unbeknownst to me, another member of my team was in hot pursuit of the receiver as well. My teammate and I realized we were both after the same prize a second too late and, unable to stop our forward momentum in time, we collided. We tumbled to the ground in a heap of arms and legs and blinding pain. When I opened my eyes, a crowd of people encircled us. They peered down with looks of sympathy mixed with horror. The school nurse shoved her way into the circle to try to assess the situation. I say try because she was dealing with a group of high school kids.

I took the opportunity of having an audience to thrust my hand in the air and wave the flag I was still proudly clutching. There were a few shouts of adulation from some other seniors. The nurse unmistakably rolled her eyes. She reached down and pried one of my eyelids farther open.

"Do you know where you are?" She asked.

"I'm pretty sure this is Hell," I remarked, to the delight of my captive audience.

She sighed and then held up three fingers. "How many fingers am I holding up?"

"She wouldn't know that anyway." A friend of mine quipped helpfully.

Chuckles rumbled through the circle of onlookers.

"I need to make sure you don't have a concussion, so I need you to answer," the nurse said, giving me a cold look. "Can you tell me your name?"

And that's when the elements of the universe aligned to afford me my perfect moment. I grinned at my friend and then looked back solemnly at the nurse and said in a clear, strong voice, "I'm… Batman."

The nurse gave up on me and moved on to assess my teammate.

They took us both to the hospital. I ended up only needing thirteen stitches, which I thought was a little underwhelming considering all the blood. I couldn't believe how much could come from that little, one-inch y-shaped cut.

⁓⌾⌾⌾⁓

I thought of that moment now as I looked at my hand, once again covered in blood from a gash in my head.

"Well I think you may have fallen and hit something on the way down. I don't think Mr. Snuggles gave you that laceration on your head. I do believe he did that though," Jim said, pointing at my leg.

My left pant leg was in shreds, with angry red scratches underneath the scraps of fabric.

"You may need some stitches for that scalp lac," Jim said in a clinical sort of way.

Jenny came charging through the door with an armful of gauze packages. She dumped them on the exam table and then came and leaned over where I was seated on the floor.

"I'm so sorry. I should have noticed that Mr. Snuggles wasn't in his cage when I checked on the animals earlier," Jenny gushed.

I tried to stand but started to wobble when I wasn't quite half way up. Jenny and Jim both stretched a hand out quickly to steady me. Once I was fully upright and swaying only slightly, Jenny let go and went to the exam table to open some of the gauze packs.

"I called Becca," Jenny said. "She said she'll be by soon and that she can take you to the hospital or home or whatever you want to do."

Rebecca was my best friend. I'd known her since I was seventeen. She was used to these types of calls – requesting rides to doctors or help getting home after an injury.

"I just want to go home. I'm sure I'll be okay." I took some of the gauze pads from Jenny and pressed them firmly to my injury to stop the bleeding.

I felt my knees weaken a bit from the pain, so I

preemptively looked for a place to sit down. Jim seemed to read my mind and pulled over a plastic chair that had been laying on its side. I took deep breaths and willed myself not to throw up again. The hard plastic was unforgiving beneath me. I shifted uncomfortably while Jenny and Jim gave me concerned side-glances.

"You sure you don't want to go to the ER just to have them check you out?" Jim asked again, his eyebrows furrowed the way they did whenever he disagreed with me.

"I'm sure. In fact, if I can get this bleeding to stop, I think I'll stay and help get this place put back together." I said, looking around at the disheveled room.

All the cabinets were open and their contents were tossed carelessly about. The jars of cotton balls and Q-tips were all upended and made it look like a blanket of snow was covering most of the counter and the surrounding floor. The biohazard bag had even been pulled from the wall and lay crumpled on the linoleum. Thankfully it looked empty.

There was a large dent in the metal garbage can that lay woefully on its side. I noticed a large, metal tripod laying across the door I entered earlier. It must have fallen (or been pushed) from its place next to the door. I always suspected that Mr. Snuggles wasn't as innocent as his name suggested.

"Don't be ridiculous," Jenny huffed, pulling me out of my ruminations. "I already called all the interns I could think of, and they're coming in to help clean up. If you won't go to the hospital then you need to go home and take it easy."

I pulled the gauze away. It was no longer white but now

a bright red. I grabbed some fresh pads and pressed them once more to my head. I had to grit my teeth to keep from crying out. I blinked back the darkness that threatened my vision from the corners of my eyes.

"Fine, I'll go home, but call me if you need anything. Anything at all," I insisted.

We heard the bell chime from the reception area, heralding an arrival or departure. I stood slowly. I was relieved to feel less dizzy this time. The room had ceased to spin, which was also a good sign. I grabbed a handful of gauze packages and followed Jenny out to reception. Jim brought up the rear. I think he was expecting me to keel over at any moment because I could feel him hovering rather close behind me.

Becca was standing, perfectly poised, in the reception area; looking around, her grey eyes widened, and her pink lips pursed. When she saw me she rushed over. "Are you okay? What happened? Who did this? They hurt you? I'll kill them!" Her words came quickly without any pauses for breath.

"I'm all right. Someone broke in, but luckily no one was here when it happened," I explained.

Becca frowned, looking back and forth between me and Jenny. "Then what happened?" Becca pointed her long, slender finger at the bloody bandage pressed to my head.

"Mr. Snuggles happened," I snarled.

Becca snorted before she could stop herself. She did her best to keep her twitching lips from evolving into a full-blown grin. I did my best to ignore her.

"I just have to get Mort, and then we can go." I brushed past my best friend and headed towards the gym.

Jenny opened her mouth to say something, but my look of death was enough to stop her.

Five minutes later, Mort and I were climbing into Becca's midnight blue, 2005 Durango. Mort needed a little boost to get into the back seat. It's a pretty tall climb for a squat bulldog. I settled into the front seat and fastened my seatbelt.

Becca checked over her shoulder before signaling and pulling out onto the street. "So he's new," Becca said, jabbing a thumb back in Mort's direction.

"Yeah, his owner dropped him off and never came back for him. You know I'm a sucker for bulldogs." I shrugged.

We sat in silence for the drive to my apartment building.

"Soooo, do you want to talk about it?" Becca asked, tucking a strand of straight, brown hair behind her ear.

I undid my seatbelt and slowly eased out of the passenger seat. I grabbed my purse and dug around inside it for my keys.

"Someone broke in again. Police say they were just looking for drugs, but they trashed the place." I spoke in a monotone.

"You don't believe them." She said it as a statement rather than a question.

"I was going through the rooms, assessing the damage, when I heard a noise. I thought maybe the burglar was still in the clinic."

"So of course you had to check it out." She rolled her eyes.

"Then I was attacked by a ferocious man-eating cat."

"Mr. Snuggles."

I ignored her interjections. "And in the struggle I was knocked unconscious. Then you showed up. The end."

I could feel her smiling, even though I wasn't looking at her. I had known her long enough to know she was trying not to laugh. I clipped the leash to Mort's thick leather collar and wrapped my arms securely around his rotund middle. He gave a little grunt and squirmed as I lowered him to the sidewalk. He offered a lingering look that I couldn't interpret and then waddled off in search of new scents to investigate.

The three of us walked through the glass-and-chrome lobby of my apartment building. Derrick the security guard gave a friendly wave as we walked past his desk. I punched the button for thirteen, and the elevator car started to rise. Some buildings don't have a 13th floor because of superstitions surrounding that number. I happened to like the number thirteen, so I didn't mind living on that floor.

"Are you feeling okay?" Becca asked, trying to make nice.

"My head hurts, but I don't feel dizzy anymore. I think it stopped bleeding."

"Well I spoke to Jim while you were back getting Mort, and he said you need to rest. If you want to take a little nap, I can wake you in an hour or so," she added meekly.

"Sure, a nap sounds good." I pulled away the fresh gauze I had pressed against my wound, it came away unsoiled.

"Then maybe we can order some take out and watch a movie or something…. If you're feeling up to it."

"Okay." I exited the elevator with Becca.

I had to tug on Mort's leash to get him off the lift before the doors closed. I frowned at him as he resisted my tugs all the way down the hallway towards my apartment. I was so concerned with his behavior that I didn't notice Becca stop short. I ran into her and gave a yelp as fresh pain from my head protested the jarring movement. Mort offered a small whimper.

"Becca, what in the world?" I yelled, immediately regretting the loud noise.

She didn't say anything. She just stepped aside, revealing my front door, slightly ajar. I felt the hair on the back of my neck stand up. My nausea came rushing full force once more upon my weakened stomach.

"What should we do?" I whispered. "Should we go in?"

"Are you nuts!?!" Becca whisper-yelled back at me. "Have you ever seen a scary movie in your life? There's no way we go in there."

"So, we just leave?"

"I'm chalking your lack of common sense up to your recent head injury, Kaly," she hissed. "We need to call the police."

She pulled out her cell phone, and I listened to the two tones as she punched the emergency number on her keypad.

"I'd like to report a break-in," she whispered into the phone.

I couldn't hear the other end of the line. I just backed slowly towards the elevator as she gave the dispatcher the address. I couldn't hear the rest of the conversation because of a loud buzzing that slowly built up in my ears. This couldn't be real. All I could think was that this was just a bad dream or that I was being filmed on a hidden camera for one of those reality TV shows. The elevator ride back to the lobby was surreal. Like I was watching myself from somewhere above, like an out-of-body experience.

Mort looked relieved to be back in the lobby. The guard, however, was not as excited about our reappearance.

"Someone broke into my apartment!" The panic made me louder than I meant to be.

"What?" Derrick shouted, jumping up from his desk and upsetting his cup of coffee.

"The door to my apartment is open, and I never leave it open," I squealed.

"That's not possible! I haven't left my post once since I came on duty at six this morning. I saw you leave, and the only non-resident we've had was a delivery guy. He didn't even go farther than the lobby. He just dropped off his package and left."

Derrick's look of offense somehow snapped me back to reality. The buzzing in my ears finally ceased, and I once more took charge of my own body.

"We called the police. They're on their way," Becca informed him.

"I'm going to go check it out," Derrick said, making a beeline for the elevator.

"They said to stay out of the apartment until they get here," Becca said, effectively bringing him to a halt.

"Oh man, oh man, oh man," Derrick muttered, running

his hand through his hair, pacing back and forth in front of the elevator.

"It'll be okay. I have renter's insurance, and I don't have anything valuable that isn't easily replaceable." I knelt down to give Mort a reassuring pat.

Mort was starting to fidget. He could sense Derrick's agitation.

"They're going to totally fire me for this." Derrick threw his hands up in the air.

"Oh, well at least you have your priorities right," Becca murmured under her breath.

The police showed up at the same time as the building manager. Becca and I waited in the lobby with Stephen, the manager, while a couple of Boston's finest went to check out my place.

"I can't believe this happened," Stephen exclaimed for the fifth time. "This is such a nice part of town. And we have a security guard here in the lobby." Stephen wrung his plump hands. His dark brown eyes glanced wildly from me to Becca and back again. "You can rest assured I fired Derrick. We'll have a better security guard here as soon as possible. And I will not leave this lobby until his replacement has arrived!"

Stephen gesticulated frantically as he spoke. He patted his sleek, black hair as though making sure it was still where it was supposed to be. "This is just so unbelievable."

"It really is," I agreed.

"Are you sure you locked your apartment when you left this morning?" he asked.

Lucky for me looks can't kill, or Stephen would be dead right now and I'd be writing this story from prison.

Stephen didn't say anything else to me while we waited for the police to finish upstairs. I did overhear him on his phone, off in a corner of the lobby. He was using enough legal terms to suggest he was talking to a lawyer. I'd worked as a witness for numerous trials over the years, and knew quite a few legal terms myself. I was a widely published expert on animal behavior, and I had also helped implement training programs for several police K9 units. I spent a fair amount of time in courtrooms talking about my expertise for judges and juries all over the country.

I hadn't even have time to contemplate a lawsuit, and Stephen was already on the phone with 1-800 please-don't-sue-me.

This was about the time the officers returned to the lobby to inform me that I had, in fact, been burglarized.

"They went through your things pretty thoroughly. Looks like they only took smaller items. It makes sense with the building having a guard in the lobby. It'd be hard to walk out of here with your flat screen and what not," Officer O'Bannon informed me in a businesslike but sympathetic tone.

"This can't be a coincidence," Becca said.

Officer O'Bannon blinked at Officer Nametag-I-couldn't-read.

"What do you mean?" O'Bannon asked.

"It can't be a coincidence that her home was robbed the same day that her clinic was robbed," Becca explained.

Officer Nametag blinked at Officer O'Bannon.

"Your clinic was robbed today?" O'Bannon said.

I nodded. "I own a veterinary clinic that was robbed last night. Now this happened," I said, pointing in the vicinity of my apartment, "sometime in the four hours I spent over there cleaning up this morning."

O'Bannon blinked at Nametag; Nametag blinked at O'Bannon.

"I think you better come down to the station and talk to one of our detectives," O'Bannon said finally.

"Can I at least see my apartment first?" I asked, on the edge of a nervous breakdown.

"Of course. I was just about to tell you, you should make a list of anything that's missing and bring it with you first thing tomorrow morning. You can ask for Detective Dwyer." O'Bannon handed me a card with his precinct's address on it.

"Something to look forward to." I couldn't hide my sarcasm.

I left the officers to their blinking and headed once more to the elevator.

CHAPTER 4
Revolving Speculations

When I walked in, I didn't even recognize my apartment. Every single thing had been moved, turned over, opened, or scattered. Becca followed me inside without making a sound. I didn't even bother taking Mort's leash off. I just dropped it and watched it drag behind him like a limp snake. He waddled around my living room, sniffing all the new smells littered across the hardwood floor.

"Aren't you going to have them at least try and dust for prints?" Becca asked, eyeing the door.

"It's gotta be the same people who broke into my clinic. They didn't leave any fingerprints there, so what's the point?" I sighed.

I turned my head slowly to assess the devastation of the entire room. I raked my fingers through my hair and blew out a slow breath. "I should be angry or sad or scared, but all I feel is confused," I admitted to my best friend.

She regarded my wrinkled brow for a moment and then started to slowly pick things up off the floor. Becca wasn't one to stand around. If she saw a problem, she fixed it. This time, however, she wasn't sure how to fix me, so she settled for fixing my savaged apartment instead.

She popped a picture back into its frame and set it on the bookshelf next to my TV. She began arranging the books that had been tipped to the floor. "I don't get it either. This is so weird," Becca said.

"Well this just proves someone is looking for something. But I have no idea who *they* are or *what* they're looking for.... Or why on earth they think I have it," I sighed again.

I walked carefully over to my antique wooden desk that sat under the windows. It used to be my favorite spot in the apartment. I loved to sit and stare at the magnificent view. To the right was an expanse of high-rise buildings, and to the left was the harbor. I used to sit for hours watching the sunlight catch on the windows and chrome of the buildings. The boats that bobbed up and down in the sparkling waters. The cars and people rushing about.

This used to be my sanctuary, my retreat, my safe place. Now, it was forever tainted by strangers. The drawers all lay open like my soul, bare and empty at the hands of derelicts who thought nothing of my privacy.

I noticed my laptop was missing, as were the flash drives I kept in my desk.

"They must have been looking for information of some kind," I said to myself.

"What?"

"Information. They must be looking for information," I said, louder this time.

Becca's eyebrows shot up, and I could read the look of uncertainty in her steel-hued eyes.

"They took my laptop and flash drives," I explained.

She gave me a lingering look and then turned back to finish arranging my bookshelf. I leaned down to pick up the papers that lay disheveled on the floor. I straightened up too fast and felt the familiar wringing twist of dizziness. I grabbed instinctively for my desk chair to keep myself from toppling over, but the chair wasn't where it should have been. It was lying on its side, on the floor. All I managed to grasp was thin air.

In all the happenings I had forgotten about my recent head injury.

Becca came running over, dodging newly created obstacles of my misplaced stuff, and helped me to my feet. "Hang onto the couch," she instructed, while she picked up the cushions from the floor.

When I was settled on the couch, Mort took that as his cue to jump up next to me and curl up for a snooze.

"Why don't you take a little nap, and I'll clean up quietly for a while," Becca suggested.

"You don't have to do that." I tried to protest, but I knew it wouldn't do any good.

I felt my eyes close involuntarily, and I drifted into darkness. The rest of the night passed quickly between stages of sleeping an hour or two at a time and cleaning for a few hours. It took until the wee hours of the morning to restore my apartment to its pre-break-in condition.

The burglars were thorough. I even discovered some

hiding places I never knew were there. The thieves left air vents open and pried up a couple loose floor boards. For the first time, I was glad there was no food in my fridge or freezer. The inconsiderate villains had left both doors open, and the insides were no longer very cold. Not that I had much of an appetite anyway.

Someone must have been watching my apartment, waiting for me to leave. I had a sense of déjà vu. It was the same feeling I had when I realized they must have been watching me at the clinic.

All through the night my mind raced with endless possibilities about who was doing this and what they were looking for. By morning I still had not come up with anything that seemed likely. Birds chirped outside my window as the sun crept up outside.

I slowly pulled my favorite sweater over my head. I was careful to avoid the gash that had just started to scab over. The sweater was a deep blue that made the blue flecks in my eyes stand out. The cashmere was soft and comforting against my skin. It was like wearing a warm hug. I slid on a pair of my favorite jeans, easing them cautiously over my bruised hip. They were dark and worn in just the right places. It had taken me a while to break them in, but now they were one of the most comfortable pieces of clothing I owned. I just needed some normalcy and comfort after everything that had happened.

Mort got excited when he saw me putting on my shoes. He made his way to the door and lay down next to it, never taking his eyes off me. I plucked up his leash. Becca must have removed it last night. Then I picked up the paper comprising "my list" that Officer O'Bannon told me to prepare. The only thing on the list was my laptop and flash drives. They were all I discovered missing throughout my search of the apartment.

I tried reconstructing everything on my computer and the drives to see if I could think of anything worth stealing. All that was on there were some patient files, my personal finances, and some vacation pictures. Nothing worth stealing and definitely nothing worth such elaborate searching.

Becca moaned and rolled over on the couch. She pulled the blanket up to her chin and squinted in my direction. "Where are you going?" she croaked.

"I'm going to drop Mort off at daycare, and then I'm going to the police station." I waved the list in the air.

"Do you want me to go with you?" She started to sit up.

"No, that's okay, I don't want you to miss any more work on my account."

"You can stay at my place tonight if you don't want to stay here alone," she suggested.

"I won't let them run me out of my own home!" I said, a little more forcefully than I meant to.

Becca started at my shout.

"Sorry," I mumbled, looking at my shoes.

"Well if you change your mind, just let me know." She relaxed back onto the sofa.

I shook my head. "Plus, you're place doesn't allow animals." I gestured down at Mort.

Becca sighed and rolled over. "Choosing a dog over your best friend." Her voice was muffled by the back of the couch, but I could still hear the smile in her voice.

"I'll call you later. Don't forget to lock up when you leave," I said on my way out the door.

I heard the soft thump of a couch pillow hitting the door behind me and couldn't help but grin. I loved that my friend understood me. She knew how I liked to make jokes when I was feeling low, even if they came at inappropriate times.

We took our time getting to the clinic. I wasn't in a hurry to get there. I was afraid of the state it would be in when I did. I was pleasantly surprised however. We walked in to find that the place looked immaculate. I would have never guessed that less than twenty-four hours ago it looked like a tornado had gone through it. I made a mental note to give Jenny a raise and buy pizza and soda for all the interns. It looked amazing, and my heart started to hurt a little less.

Jenny looked up from her desk after the bell announced my arrival. She smiled with pride when she noticed my impressed expression.

"Looks good as new doesn't it?" she beamed.

"It's fantastic, Jenny. I don't know how to thank you." I breathed.

"I know. We did really great work!" she said.

"I just came to drop Mort off, and then I need to head down to the police station to talk with a detective about what happened." I purposely left out any mention of the break-in at my apartment. There was no need to ruin her good mood.

"Okay. Let me know if they need to talk to me. I was the

first one here after all." She seemed a little disappointed that they hadn't asked her to come in too.

"I'm sure they just asked me because I own the clinic," I fibbed.

She seemed to buy my excuse.

"Oh, a technician from the alarm company came by," Jenny said.

"What?"

She caught the confusion in my face, so she explained. "I called them to come check the system. I know you set that thing religiously, so I thought maybe there was something wrong on their end."

I made a mental note to give her an even bigger raise. The thought hadn't even crossed my mind.

In a hushed voice Jenny continued. "They said someone cut the wires."

My eyes widened. I didn't think anything else could shock me after all that had happened the past two days, but for some reason this information did.

"The alarm guy said it had to be a pro. No one else would know how to disable their system like that," Jenny added with a flourish, obviously pleased she had extracted this bit of intel.

I was speechless. This was one more detail that made no sense. I felt like I was trying to put a puzzle together, but all the pieces were flipped over. I kept getting more and more pieces, but I still had no idea how they fit together or what the picture on the other side was supposed to be. "I guess I'll let the police know when I talk to them," I said.

Jenny just shrugged her shoulders and went back to whatever she had been working on before I arrived.

I dropped Mort off and then caught a bus that stopped near the address Officer O'Bannon gave me. I stared briefly at the white stone of District F-14's small station. Though it wasn't very large, it was still a formidable looking building. I couldn't imagine what it would be like to come here on the opposite side of the law. Even being a law-abiding citizen, I felt intimidated just standing here.

The revolving glass doors found the sun every time they moved. The light danced around the street as the door spun in hypnotic circles. Taking a deep breath, I finally worked up the courage to enter the station.

⋘⋘⋙⋙

I should warn you now that I have a history with revolving doors. On more than one occasion I have found myself stuck in them. I have a knack for finding inventive ways of stopping all forward motion.

⋘⋘⋙⋙

Today was no exception. I knocked a piece of wayward garbage into the slot with me. I was a couple steps from exiting the circulating doors when I stepped on the refuse, causing my foot to shoot out from under me. The force of my sliding foot was enough to wedge the debris under the door, which could now stop a rhinoceros. Inertia then carried the top part of my body forward rather violently. I face-planted into the glass about two feet up from the push handle.

To add insult to my injured pride, a couple other bumps reverberated through the door. That's when I knew that my luck for jamming revolving doors had trapped two other people as well. It took a few awkward moments to extricate us all from the situation, but I forgot about it almost as soon as I was free.

It felt as though I had been transported to a new world when I entered the lobby. The bustle of police officers and alleged criminals in handcuffs moved to a rhythm all their own. Phones rang, desk chairs squeaked, slurred profanity rang out from somewhere to my left. It was enough to make me forget the embarrassment of yet another door trapping.

I walked hesitantly up to the front desk. I waited while an overworked man massaged his temples. He listened morosely to the person in line in front of me. When it was finally my turn, I gave him my name and told him I was there to see Detective Dwyer. I explained that Officer O'Bannon told me to come in and speak to the detective first thing this morning.

The exhausted desk worker didn't say a word to me. He just picked up the closest phone and paged Detective Dwyer. Then he pointed a finger to some chairs nearby and turned his attention to the person in line behind me.

I was about to ask how long it might be when the person behind me, reeking of garlic, shoved me to the side. I sat meekly on the edge of one of the wooden chairs he'd ordered me to. I was afraid to touch anything. I can be a bit of a germaphobe if I let my mind dwell on such things.

I waited there twenty minutes before my name was finally called. A man I assumed was Detective Dwyer swaggered into the lobby. My assumption proved correct when he extended a hand and introduced himself. He ushered me back through the crowded station. Our journey ended in a private office off to the right.

He didn't waste any time, he just jumped right into it. "Thanks for coming down. I have Officer O'Bannon's report here in front of me." He looked down at a plain, tan folder opened before him. "He says you had both your place of business and your home broken into within twenty-four hours of one another. Is that correct?" His voice was gruff and lacked any semblance of compassion.

"Yes. First my vet clinic and then my apartment," I explained.

"You work in a veterinary clinic?"

"Yes. Actually, I own the clinic. I'm the head vet there as well," I answered.

"Do you ever take any of your *work* home with you?"

The way he said work sent up red flags in my mind.

"Well, sometimes I take patient charts home if I'm behind in writing out my notes," I said hesitantly.

"Is there anything else you take home from the clinic? Equipment, biological samples, *medication* perhaps?" He didn't take his eyes off me for a second.

"Absolutely not!" I was horrified at his insinuations. "I've never taken any of the drugs home. They always stay locked up at the clinic, and we keep extensive records of them. My office manager gave the police a copy of all our records when they came to investigate. If you look at them, you'll see that we are very careful with inventory." I tried to keep my tone even.

He was just doing his job. I shouldn't have been upset that he was covering all his bases. Of course he thought this was about drugs. What else could he think it was about?

"I don't think this is about drugs," I said defensively.

Dwyer's eyebrows went up. "Oh really? And what do you think this is about?"

"I don't know, but whoever broke in was looking for something, and it wasn't drugs," I stated hotly.

"Weren't there drugs taken?" Dwyer said accusingly.

"Well, yes they were, but the way they went through everything…. I'm not exaggerating when I tell you they searched *everything*. If it was just about drugs, why didn't they stop when they found the drug cabinet? And why would they go to my home too? That doesn't make any sense." I waved my hands helplessly.

Dwyer didn't say anything for a moment. Then he asked, "What was missing from your home?"

I handed him my list. He looked at it and flipped it over. He frowned and then flipped it back to the front again.

"This is it?" He waved it at me.

"That's it," I said firmly.

He turned his head and looked at me sideways. "What kind of information did you keep on your laptop?"

"Patient records, financial records, and some personal

things like vacation photos and some emails," I answered.

"We're going to need a list of your clients," he said after some thought.

"I'll have to talk to my lawyer first and make sure there are no confidentiality issues, but I don't think that will be a problem," I said.

He squinted at me. "Can you think of anything someone might have been after? If they were, in fact, after something other than drugs?"

I shook my head. "I have been racking my brain, but I can't think of anything."

"What about any changes to your work life?" he asked.

"I hired a new vet to help me with my workload, but that was a while ago. Other than that, nothing has changed," I said.

Dwyer tilted his head. "What about your personal life? Any changes there?"

"I got a new dog." I shrugged. "Other than that, I haven't had any changes."

I don't know why this confession embarrassed me. Maybe because Dwyer rolled his eyes when I mentioned Mort. Maybe I thought he was judging my personal life.

"Sorry I'm not more exciting," I sneered.

Dwyer didn't answer. He just shuffled some papers around. He gave a quiet sigh and closed the folder. I knew then that he was giving up. "Thank you for coming in. If you think of anything else, please give me a call." He handed me a card with his name and number on it.

"That's it?!" I squeaked.

"We will keep the file open, but without more to go on, there's really nothing else we can do right now. I'm sorry." His voice didn't sound very sincere.

"The alarm company said someone cut the wires for the alarm system!" I blurted out desperately.

In my intimidated state, this fact had slipped my mind completely until now. Dwyer frowned and opened the folder to jot down a note on one of the pages.

"Send me the contact info for your alarm company, and I'll give them a call," he said.

I think it was more to placate me than because it would amount to anything.

I sighed. "Okay."

Dwyer stood and stuck out his hand once more. I reluctantly shook it and followed his gestured command to exit his office.

He pointed back the way we had come. "Do you need me to walk you out?" His tone was dismissive.

"No, I can manage," I said weakly.

He didn't say anything else. He just sat back down in his chair. I stepped out of sight next to his door. I needed a minute to get my heart to stop racing, but I didn't want Dwyer to see me. As I stood there, I couldn't help but overhear him talking on the phone.

"Yeah, I just met with her." There was a pause, then he continued. "It's just drug seekers. There's no point in wasting any more time or effort on it. I'll keep it in my drawer just in case, but I'd bet money that she got mixed up with the wrong drug buyer."

Anger bubbled up inside me, but it was mixed with hopelessness. If I thought about it, I couldn't really blame the detective for thinking that. At the same time I was mad because I knew it wasn't true. I walked slowly back through the maze of desks. There was no point obsessing over it.

Utterly defeated, I headed back to the clinic. Unless something happened that could point me in the right direction, there was really nothing else to be done. I would soon regret wishing for something to happen.

CHAPTER 5
A Bulldog's Intuition

Over the next month, I threw myself into my work. If I stopped too long to think, my mind would always end up back in an endless loop of possibilities trying to explain the break-ins. I also kept getting a funny feeling I couldn't shake. Becca told me it was just some kind of psychological trauma from the break-ins, but it sure seemed like something more than that. I couldn't put my finger on it. I didn't get the feeling all the time, just every once in a while. It would make my skin crawl. It got so bad that I think Mort picked up on it too and would get a bit antsy.

Thankfully there were no more incidents, though I don't know where else they could have searched, even if they'd wanted to. They'd gone over everything I owned with a fine-tooth comb. Perhaps it was their violation of my privacy that made me feel so creeped out all the time. I even hired a company to sweep my apartment for recording devices. I'm still a little embarrassed to admit it. I couldn't sleep one night, and I saw an infomercial for the company, so I called and made an appointment.

Becca laughed when I told her, but Jenny asked to have them come to the clinic next. And yes, I had them check the clinic too. Jenny threatened to quit if I didn't.

Jenny had always been into conspiracy theories, so I wasn't really surprised by her demand. I was, however, a little surprised at my own paranoia. I blamed it on the creepy feeling I kept getting.

I had the feeling again as Mort and I were walking home. The sun had gone down more than an hour ago. The streetlights were on, but they were outnumbered by shadows. Every dark corner looked ominous. I walked a little faster. Mort picked up on my unrest. He pulled me to the edge of some bushes under which he then cowered and refused to come out. I crawled under the bush to help coax him out. Soon the two of us were covered in mud, but Mort wouldn't budge.

That's when I heard a twig snap nearby, and my heart stopped. I had my arm wrapped around Mort's portly mid-section, and I could feel him trembling, or maybe I was the one trembling. I couldn't tell for sure. I fumbled in my pocket, trying to find the can of pepper spray I always carry for when I have to walk home at night. I pulled it out quietly and put my unsteady finger on the depressor.

"I thought she came this way. Didn't she come this way?" said the first voice. It was a soft baritone.

"Well do ya see her anywhere?" The second voice said in a nasally, irritating voice.

"I don't understand. We should've seen if she turned

somewhere," The baritone replied.

"You musta missed it, cause she sure didn't go this way," Dweeby voice number two chided.

"I didn't miss it."

"Right, so her and her dog are just hidin' in the bushes somewhere for no reason?!" Nasal man shrieked.

"Don't be an idiot. They're not in the bushes. You just lost them. Let's go back and try to find where they turned."

My heart started thumping louder. Were they looking for me? I didn't recognize their voices. If they were looking for me, why weren't they calling my name? The bad feeling I'd been having grew steadily worse. Mort gave a soft whimper. I instinctively put my hand over his mouth, which in hindsight was pointless and stupid, but in the moment it felt like the thing to do.

"What was that?" Baritone man asked quietly.

Footsteps came closer. The bushes next to me rustled softly. I clamped a hand over my own mouth to keep from crying out. I squeezed my eyes shut as the footsteps grew louder. They were almost in front of the bush I was under. I stopped breathing. I opened my eyes just in time to see something small and furry dart out of the bush next to me. It ran across the sidewalk and out into the street.

Lucky for me Dweeby screams like a girl. It was enough to cover the small yelp I involuntarily gave. A glance at Mort told me he couldn't be bothered with whatever fluffy creature had just vacated its hiding spot next to us. I bit down on my lip while I listened to baritone man wheeze with laughter.

"Let's get outta here, I don't wanna get rabies or somethin'." Dweeby sulked and stomped off.

His petulant stomps faded in the distance. I waited until it was quiet for a few moments before I let out the breath I was holding. Mort licked my face and then crawled out from under the bush. I shook my head and then crawled out after him.

"You're getting a nice juicy burger for dinner," I whispered as we started to jog home.

We were crossing the street in front of my apartment when my maladroit tendencies once more reminded me of who I am. I wish I could blame it on a pothole that I didn't see, or getting tangled in Mort's leash. The truth is I sometimes just forget how to walk. I felt myself fall in slow motion, wondering how I managed to trip on nothing yet again. Then pain flared all over my body as I hit the pavement with multiple appendages. If dogs can roll their eyes, Mort rolled his at me as I carefully peeled myself up off the blacktop.

I must have been a sight for poor Phil, the new security guard at my building. His eyes were wide when he caught site of me through the door.

"Hey Phil, do you happen to have a first aid kit? I could really use some Band-Aids," I said.

"Oh man, what happened to you?!"

"I fell," I replied.

"Down some stairs?" he asked.

"No, just in the street, on my way here." I jabbed a thumb back at the street behind me.

"And then you got hit by a car?"

"What the…? No, I just fell!" I was trying to remain calm.

"Are you sure you didn't get hit by a car?"

"I think I'd remember it if I did," I said indignantly.

"Not if he hit you hard enough," he reasoned.

"Can I please just have some Band-Aids?"

"Oh, yeah, I don't have a first aid kit." Phil shrugged.

I dropped my head to my chest. "Of course you don't."

Mort and I trudged up to the apartment. The first order of business once safely ensconced (my new deadbolt firmly slid into place) was to give Mort a bath. He was caked in mud after our game of hide-n-seek under the bushes. I would have liked to clean myself up first, but he wasn't one to sit still while I tended to my wounds. I caught him midair as he tried to jump onto my clean couch, so I carried the sullied bulldog into the bathroom. I was concerned that he might not like baths. As I tested the water with my fingers, I realized I didn't need to worry.

No sooner had I turned on the water then he had jumped into the tub all by himself. I pulled off his beautiful leather collar just in time to keep it from getting wet. Never before had I seen a dog who loved a bath more than Mort. I could have sworn he was drooling as I worked the shampoo into a lather. He gave a little sigh that melted my heart as I rinsed him clean with the warm water from my detachable shower head. I toweled him off, and then threw a dry towel on the ground for him to lay on while I took a quick shower.

Once we were both clean, I called Becca to tell her about

what happened on my way home.

"Did you call the police?!" she asked, after I had finished recapping my eventful walk.

"And say what exactly? That I think I was being followed, but I'm not sure because I was in the bushes with my dog?"

Becca was silent for a moment. "Sooo, you're not going to do anything?"

"I don't know what to do!" I shouted.

Silence.

I sighed. "Sorry. I feel like I'm losing my mind. Am I losing my mind?"

"No," Becca said. "We both know you can't lose something you never had to begin with."

We both started laughing, and the tension eased.

Then she got serious again. "Do you want me to come over?"

I thought about it, then answered, "No, I'm just going to order dinner and watch some TV. I'll be all right."

"Okay." She didn't sound convinced. "Call me tomorrow?"

"Sure thing."

I pressed end, and then went to the kitchen to look through my stack of menus from nearby restaurants. I ordered my dinner from the only place in the neighborhood that delivered burgers. I made sure to order their half-pound Angus burger for Mort. Then I used the house phone to call down to Phil. I asked him to give me a call when my food came. I didn't want anyone coming up to my door. If he thought it was an odd request he hid it well.

Twenty minutes later he called to summon me to the lobby. I heard some shouting in the background, and a chill went down my spine. I recognized the nasally tenor voice from earlier that evening. I hung up and stared at my phone for a moment, unsure of what to do. Then a mixture of bravery and/or stupidity washed over me, and I grabbed my cell phone.

When I got to the lobby, I did my best to take the "delivery" man's picture while pretending to text. I wasn't sure what was about to happen, but I at least wanted some sort of proof. I quickly texted it to Becca in case something happened to me, then I swore off all the detective shows I had ever watched. I'm not sure if I was being really smart or really paranoid. Is it crazy to hope you're being paranoid?

"I woulda brought it up to you, but this steroid usin' mall cop wouldn't let me," Dweeby whined. "This better not affect my tip."

The more he spoke, the more certain I was it was the same guy from earlier.

"It won't," I said quickly.

I tried to keep my hand from shaking as I handed him some money. As soon as I had my food, I turned towards the elevator.

"Keep the change," I said over my shoulder.

I hid around the corner and waited about five minutes before poking my head out to make sure the coast was clear. When I saw the empty lobby, I called Phil over to me.

"Um, is everything all right, Ms. Aiton?" Phil's dark eyebrows were nearly to his hairline.

"That man, if you ever seen him again…. I don't ever want him let upstairs. Okay? Not for any reason," I said in a low voice.

"Why, did he do something to you?" The alarm was growing in Phil's voice.

"He was following me earlier. I don't think he's really a delivery guy." I tried to keep the irrational lunatic sound out of my tone.

"If he's following you we should call the police," Phil said and turned back to his desk.

I grabbed him. "No!" I shouted. I cleared my throat and spoke a little quieter. "It's okay. There's a detective investigating the break-in at my apartment. I'll let him know. We don't need the police here again."

That's the last thing I needed, another police visit. The neighbors were still unsettled from their last visit a month ago. No, I would just call Detective Dwyer and let him know what happened. Maybe even send him the picture I took. Perhaps then he'd believe that this was about something other than drugs.

I got back to my apartment and was greeted by a very hungry Mort. He followed the bag of food I was holding all the way to the kitchen. I pulled the Angus burger off its bun and scraped away the ketchup. I chopped it up and mixed it in with a bit of his dry dog food. As Mort happily scarfed his well-deserved dinner, I hunted down Detective Dwyer's business card and tapped his number on my phone. I was expecting to leave him a message, since it was well after business hours, so I was surprised when he answered.

"Detective Dwyer." His agitated voice startled me.

"Um, yes, hello Detective Dwyer. This is Kaly. Kaly Aiton?"

"Who?"

"Kaly Aiton. I'm the veterinarian who had her clinic and home broken into about a month ago."

"Oh, right. I'm sorry, Ms. Aiton, there's nothing new to report on your case," he said.

"No, that's not why I'm calling. Well, I guess it's kind of why I'm calling. It's just that, I don't know how else to say this, but I think I'm being followed." It all came spilling out of my mouth. "Two men followed me after work. I didn't see their faces, but I heard their voices. Then later, a man showed up at my apartment with the food I ordered, but he wasn't wearing a delivery outfit and I recognized his voice as one of the men who was following me."

Silence.

"Detective Dwyer?"

"I'm still here. You're sure it was the same person? Voices can sound alike Ms. Aiton," he suggested.

"He has a very distinctive voice, Detective," I retorted.

"So you don't know who the man is?" he asked.

"I have absolutely no idea. I don't recognize him."

Another silence.

"I… I took a picture of him with my cell phone. I can send it to you. Maybe that would help?"

Dwyer sighed. "Sure, go ahead and send it. I'll put it in your file. But I have to be honest, without an ID I don't know if a photo will help much."

I rubbed my forehead. I don't know what I was expecting, but I had at least hoped for something more than that.

Dwyer seemed to sense my frustration, and his voice softened a bit. "I'm really sorry, Ms. Aiton. I wish there were something else I could do. My only advice is to keep an eye out. If you see the man again, call us right away and we can try to get someone to come by and pick him up. Maybe we can get some answers then."

I nodded slowly, then realized I was on the phone. "Okay."

I hung up, dejected. I looked at the cold burger and fries I had set out on a plate before I started the call. Suddenly I wasn't feeling very hungry. I dumped the food into the garbage and went to recheck the locks on my front door. It had become somewhat of a compulsive habit to check them five or six times a night. As an added precaution, I wedged one of my dining chairs under the doorknob like I'd seen people do in the movies. Then I headed into my bedroom.

Mort followed me as I went through my nightly ritual of getting ready for bed. I thought about calling Becca and asking her to come over, but when I looked at the clock I thought better of it. I tried reading a few pages from the novel on my nightstand but found myself reading the same sentence over and over. I couldn't make my brain comprehend what I was reading, no matter how many times my eyes traveled over the words.

I gave up and burrowed deeper under my warm, faux-down comforter. Mort curled up next to me. He didn't seem to care that I had a king-size bed. He always had to be right up by my side. It was like he couldn't fall asleep unless he was leaned up against me. Tonight, I didn't mind.

I lay awake for more than an hour, thinking about everything that had happened. Replaying everything again and again in my mind. Both break-ins, the walk home, and the food delivery. I studied the man's picture on my phone, trying to remember if I had ever seen him anywhere before. None of it made sense. I still couldn't fathom who would do this or why they would target me.

Every time I was on the verge of falling asleep, I would imagine I heard the front door rattling and I would bolt upright in bed, heart pounding, palms sweating. I would listen intently for a few moments until I convinced myself that I was just imagining it, and I would finally lay back down. As a last resort, I turned on the TV. I flipped through the channels looking for something light and funny to distract me. I finally fell asleep watching re-runs of *Saturday Night Live.*

I awoke from a deep sleep to the sound of my cell phone blaring unnaturally loud in my ear. The sun poured through the windows in-between the curtains I had forgotten to close the night before.

"Where are you?" A frantic voice asked. "Kaly! Where are you?!"

CHAPTER 6
Courthouse Tumbling

I was in such a deep sleep that it took me a moment to recognize the voice. It was Becca. In all my years of knowing her, she had never sounded so scared.

"Becca?" I mumbled, trying to fight off the gnawing sense of anxiety that was growing inside me.

"Kaly! Are you at home? Can you come over? He was here. I woke up and he was here, going through my things." She spoke so quickly it sounded like one word without any pauses.

"Who was there, Becca? What are you talking about?"

"That man, the one from the picture you sent me! Why was he in my apartment, Kaly? Why was he going through my stuff? Who is he?" She was crying.

I sat up so fast I nearly rolled Mort right off the bed. All memory of sleep fled from the terror that now filled my heart.

"Call the police, Becca. Call them right now," I instructed, untangling my legs from my sheets.

"I already did. They're here now trying to get fingerprints."

I gave the biggest sigh of my life. I put the phone on speaker so I could throw on some clothes while we talked. "And you're sure it was the guy from the photo?" I asked.

"I'm sure. I saw him and screamed. I think it caught him off guard because he stared at me for what felt like forever before he ran off." She sobbed quietly around her words.

"I'll call that detective from my case. Maybe this will light a fire under him. Maybe now he'll believe me that it isn't about drugs." My voice muffled as I pulled on a shirt.

"Can you just come over please? I need someone here right now," she begged.

"Of course. I'm on my way now. I'll see you soon."

I rushed out of the bedroom with Mort on my heels. I frantically tied my shoelaces as I went. I only fell down twice. I went to snap Mort's leash on when I realized he wasn't wearing his collar. I didn't want to waste any more time, so I looped the leash around his neck and secured it to itself. Mort did great on a leash, so I wasn't too worried about it.

I was just about to rush out the door when my phone rang again. "Hello?" I answered breathlessly, not bothering to see who it was.

"Kaly? Where are you?" Jenny's voice crackled through my phone.

I felt my heart drop in my chest. "Not again," I whispered.

"Did you just fall?" Jenny asked impatiently.

"What? No, Jenny, I didn't. Why are you calling? What happened?"

"What happened is you were supposed to meet with the prosecutor's office an hour ago to go over your testimony for that trial this afternoon. They just called looking for you," she informed me.

I took in a sharp breath. "Oh no! I totally forgot!"

"That's why I was calling you. It's not like you to forget something like that. Are you okay?" Jenny sounded genuinely concerned.

"Someone broke into Becca's place. She just called. She wants me to come over, but I'm supposed to be in court soon." At this point I made some sort of unflattering, grunting noise that doesn't really translate into words.

"Someone broke into her place? Like they broke in here?" Jenny's voice went up an octave.

"Yeah," I said through clenched teeth.

I raced back to my closet to grab the suit I had picked out a few days ago. After grabbing the shoebox sitting under the suit, I raced once more to the door of my apartment. Luckily I saw my briefcase packed with my notes and my PowerPoint sitting next to the door, or I would have forgotten it too.

"That can't possibly be a coincidence, can it?" Jenny whispered.

"No, it was the same guy who followed me home last night. It's no coincidence," I said, fumbling with my keys, trying to lock my door with a shaky hand.

"What?!?" Jenny screeched, forcing me to drop my phone in self-defense of my eardrum.

I scooped up my phone, dropping my shoebox in the

process. Mort dove out of the way just in time. I tried a couple times to pick up the box, but the leash, suit, briefcase, and my phone made it impossible, so I just kicked the box towards the elevator.

"Look, can you just meet me at Becca's? I told her I would come by. I'll just change once I get there and head straight for court, but I need you to come get Mort," I pleaded.

Jenny sighed. She always pretended to hate drama, but I knew she loved being in the middle of it.

"Is it safe to go over there?" She inquired.

"The police are there now, so it's fine," I said impatiently.

"Fine, I'll be there in a little bit," she huffed.

Once on the ground floor, I scooted my shoebox to the guard's desk. The bewildered morning guard picked up the shoebox and tucked it under my arm for me.

"Thanks, Dean," I said over my shoulder.

"No problem. Have a nice day!" he called after me.

We made it three blocks before we were halted by a red light. I didn't see the man approach until he was only a few feet away. He closed the distance quickly, and before I could say anything he was kneeling down next to Mort and scratching him behind the ears. Mort gave a low growl, which was more than I could get out. I just stood there speechless.

"Nice dog you've got here." It was the baritone man from the day before.

I just stared at him and nodded dumbly. Mort gave a louder growl as the man frisked him. I use the word frisk because there's no other word I can think of to describe what happened. It was like one of those TSA people in the airport and Mort was a suspicious looking passenger. The man ran his hands around the leash too, eyeing it closely.

"He's a bulldog right?" the man asked, looking up at me after he had finished his search.

Again, all I could do was nod. My heart pounded, and my hands began to sweat.

"Bulldogs are the best," he said.

With that, the light turned green, the walk light lit up, and the man crossed the street in front of us. Mort and I remained motionless. When my wits finally returned, I lead Mort across the street and then in a different direction than the one the man had taken. It took us a little longer to get to Becca's by going that way, but I wanted to put as much distance between us and the man as I could.

I didn't tell Becca what happened; she had enough going on already. The police were just leaving when I arrived. I made some tea while Becca told me her story from the beginning. There wasn't much more to it than what she'd told me over the phone. I left a message for Detective Dwyer and then got dressed for court.

I hated leaving Becca at a time like this, but it couldn't be helped. Being an expert in animal behavior and all my training with K9s for the special police units, I was often called to give testimony for court cases involving animals. This case was particularly gruesome, involving a man who ran a dog fighting ring.

One of his dogs attacked a child, and the prosecution

wanted to go after the owner. They asked me to come and testify about how a dog can be trained for aggression. It was the kind of case I loved to testify for. It broke my heart to see animals punished for their owners actions, and I especially abhorred dog fighting. I wanted to do whatever I could to bring the scumbag to justice.

When I finished my testimony, the prosecutor gave me a triumphant smile and nod as I left the stand. It was just what I needed. I left the courtroom feeling like I was finally back in control of something in my life. For once there was something I could do. Something I could do well. It replaced the hopeless feeling I had been nursing for the last month. I was confident that the judge and jury would see things my way and punish the man to the full extent of the law. I was walking down the hall, basking in the glow of my triumph, feeling truly proud of myself.

And that's when I saw him.

I don't know how I recognized him after only seeing the back of his head. Maybe because I had been subconsciously looking for him ever since he failed to show up to get Mortimer.

"Henry?!" I called out.

The man froze but didn't turn around. I knew then that it was him.

"Henry!" I called out, louder this time.

He started walking briskly away from me without turning around. I repeated his name, louder and louder until he finally stopped. His shoulders sagged, and he turned slowly to face me.

The first thing out of his mouth was, "How's Mort?"

"Do you even care?!" I spat.

"I know you don't understand why I did that, but I had to, and I can't explain why."

The pain in his voice softened my anger by a few degrees.

"Well you can make up for it by coming to pick him up now." I said, not yet ready to forgive and forget.

"I wish I could, but he's safer with you."

This set off alarm bells in my head.

"What does that mean?" I couldn't mask my look of horror.

"There are dangerous people after me. I can't stay in one place for long, so Mort is better off with you. You can give him a permanent, safe place to live and a good life that he deserves."

I wanted to be angry with him, but his sincerity was so touching.

"Dangerous people? What like the mafia or loan sharks or something?" I couldn't help the mocking tone that permeated my words.

Henry shook his head. "I can't explain it. You wouldn't believe me. But that doesn't change the fact that it's true. I'm sorry."

"So you're just going to leave him to be stuck in a cage every night until I can find some family to adopt him?" I felt my sympathy melt and my anger bubble back to the surface.

It was his turn to look horrorstruck. "You wouldn't do that would you?"

The confusion must have been evident on my face

because he continued without further prompting. "You'll keep him won't you? He can keep going home with you and spending his days at your daycare. He really likes it there," he said.

I stood dumbfounded for a few moments. Henry glanced around the crowded courthouse hallway.

"How did you know I take him home with me?" I whispered.

"I... I...," he stammered.

"Have you been watching me?!?"

"When we met, you seemed like a really good person, plus you're a vet. I thought you'd take good care of him if I left him, but I had to make sure. Mort means a lot to me, so I may have... I may have watched to make sure you would take care of him. Once or twice?" He shrugged helplessly, and a blush crept up his cheeks.

"If you care about him then you shouldn't have abandoned him!" I was shouting now. I just couldn't help myself, this whole situation was too bizarre and overwhelming.

Henry's head whipped around as he took in our surroundings for the third time. "Like I said, I don't expect you to understand, but I do expect you to take care of Mort. Please? I'm begging you. He's a good dog. Give him a good home. If money's an issue I'll send some. I just need to know that you're going to take good care of him." The pleading in his voice again threatened my justifiable rage.

"You need help, you know that?!" I exclaimed in frustration.

To my surprise he laughed. "I'm painfully aware."

"I can recommend a few professionals you could talk to." I felt my anger slip at the sound of his laugh.

"They don't train therapists for this kind of thing." His smile was tinged with sadness.

Before I could say anything else, he spun on his heel and took off down the hall.

"Wait, you aren't leaving are you?" I called after him.

He didn't stop, he just kept walking. So I did the only reasonable thing I could think of and took off after him. He was halfway down the stairs by the time I reached them. I followed after him, but going down stairs in high heeled shoes is not an easy task, even by skilled professionals. And I'm, well, me.

I realized I was falling before it actually happened. A thought flashed through my head, in images rather than words. If I didn't lose my shoes I was going to, at best, break my ankle, at the very worst break my ever-loving neck. So with the reflexes of a ninja and the grace of a flailing newborn pony, I managed to kick off my shoes as I tumbled/slid down the remaining steps inside the courthouse.

I miraculously ended up at the bottom of the stairs on my feet. In the adrenaline infused, brain fart of the moment, I noticed a group of people waiting on the benches along the hallway I had landed in. Feeling all eyes on me, I did the only natural thing I could do: I gave one of those gymnastics poses, gathered my shoes and briefcase, and walked out of the courthouse to the sound of applause.

My body is so used to being in embarrassing situations, through some sort of evolutionary adaptation it instinctually knows how to downplay the humiliation.

It's funny the things that pop into your head when you're facing your own mortality. As I was close to breaking my neck on the way down the stairs, it finally occurred to me: Henry was the only thing different in my life. Ever since Henry had shown up, strange men kept breaking into places connected to me.

He had to be the reason this was all happening. I thought about how he'd said he was in danger and that I wouldn't understand. That just made me think I was right in my conclusion. I *had* to find Henry. I had to make him explain it all to me. Mostly, I just really needed to know what those men were looking for.

I ran out onto the sidewalk and looked both ways. There were people everywhere. It would be difficult to find him amidst this sea of humanity.

"Henry!" I shouted.

It had worked last time, maybe it would work again.

"Henry!"

But aside from the weird looks of passersby, there was no other response.

I slipped my shoes back on and started walking towards the bus stop. Lost in thought, I walked slowly towards my destination. I made a list of possibilities for who could be after Henry. Loan sharks? International arms dealers? A ring of jewel thieves? My imagination ran wild with speculation.

I didn't notice the movement out of the corner of my eye

until it was too late. A hand clasped over my mouth. Then a strong arm dragged me into an alleyway, and there was nothing I could do to stop it from happening.

CHAPTER 7
Near-Death Déjà Vu

For the second time in a matter of minutes, I could picture my imminent demise. I've had more than my fair share of near-death experiences, but they're usually more spread out. I didn't see my life flash before my eyes, but I did have a flashback of the time I was visiting missionary friends who lived on a small island in the Caribbean.

We were spending the day at a picturesque beach, famous for its two to three story tall boulders that sat along its shoreline. The boulders created tunnels along the beach. Crystal clear water over powder white sand made up the "floors" of the tunnels. The water was anywhere from knee high to shoulder deep and led in so many directions, we spent most of the day exploring. We climbed the boulders to discover a place where we could jump into the calm but deep waters of the turquois ocean.

This was where a friend led me not long after lunch. We were nearly to the top when my foot missed a step and I slipped down the steep incline of the boulder. My knees and hands scraped and grasped desperately for purchase, anything to slow my deadly descent. Finally I managed to grab hold of a crevice and end my heart-pounding plummet. My friend scrambled over as quickly as he could to help haul me back up. If I had continued my downward journey, I would have fallen to my death on the jagged rocks two stories below.

I thought of my friend's strong hand pulling me back up to safety and compared it to the strong hand that pulled me into the alley. They felt entirely different. My friend's hand had felt reassuring, confident, safe. This hand felt menacing, devious, wrong.

"I have a gun. If you scream, I will shoot you. Nod if you understand," said a voice I immediately recognized.

I nodded slowly. My knees knocked together. I always thought that was just a figure of speech; it's not. Baritone man turned me around, and for the first time I noticed he wasn't alone. Nasal man was there too. Both of them were pointing guns at me. I felt my heart skip a beat.

"How do you know Henry?" Baritone growled.

"H… Henry?" I stammered.

"Yes, we heard you calling his name when you came out of the courthouse. Tell us everything, or this won't end well for you." He shoved his gun into my ribs.

Tears welled in my eyes. "I don't really know him. He just left his dog at my veterinary clinic. I couldn't just leave his poor dog there, so I took him home with me until Henry came back for him," I whimpered.

"Why was he here then? Why were you chasing after him?" Nasal man asked.

"I saw him in the courthouse and asked him if he was coming back for his dog," I said, trying to stop my tears and slow my breathing.

"What else?" Baritone persisted.

"He asked how his dog was. That was it, I swear," I finally managed to say through hiccups and sobs.

"You expect us to believe that?" Nasal man sneered.

"I don't know what else you're expecting, but that's all we talked about. I... I yelled at him for abandoning his dog. He told me to take good care of him. Then he ran out, and I came running after him," I blubbered.

"Stop right there!" a voice yelled.

The three of us whipped our heads around. I may have cried out in joy, or I may have just thought about doing it, but standing there with his gun drawn was Detective Dwyer. I've never been so glad to see anyone in my life.

"Boston P.D. Put down your guns, both of you, now!" he ordered.

I'd like to say it was purely self-preservation that made me hit the ground when the bullets started flying. But if I'm being completely honest, when the first shot was fired, it made me jump. I landed wrong and couldn't regain my balance. It was the first time my maladroitness saved my life.

When the shooting stopped, I carefully lifted my head from behind a garbage can. Baritone man was lying on the ground. He wasn't moving. Detective Dwyer was sitting up against one of the alley walls. He had his hand clasped to his shoulder. I could see blood spreading underneath his crimson-smeared hand. The rest of the alley was empty.

"You're shot," I said and scrambled over to him.

"You should be a detective. Your powers of observation are so astute," he said through gritted teeth.

"Let me see," I instructed, slipping into emergency doctor mode.

He shrunk back. "You're not a real doctor."

I rolled my eyes. "I'm not a *human* doctor, but I know how to triage a wound. Now shut up and let me see it," I commanded.

He moved his hand to reveal the entrance wound just below his left collar bone. He was lucky. A few inches lower and it could have punctured his heart. I pulled off my jacket and ripped it in half. I pressed it over the hole to stop the bleeding. I leaned him forward and found the exit wound. I pressed the other half of my jacket over it to staunch the bleeding there as well.

"Keep this pressed firmly. It will help stop the bleeding. The bullet went all the way through so I'm mostly worried about getting the bleeding to stop. Where's the other guy?" I asked.

Detective Dwyer placed a shaking hand to the wad of cloth pressed against his shoulder. I continued to keep pressure on his back and reached for the phone clipped to his belt.

"He ran. My partner went after him," Dwyer said with a grimace.

I dialed 911 and waited for an answer. "You need to send an ambulance, an officer's been shot. We're in the alley next to the courthouse."

I dropped the phone when I saw Dwyer lose consciousness. I pressed the cloth he had dropped back to his shoulder and waited for the ambulance to arrive. Moments later his partner came running up, out of breath.

"Is he...?" His partner dropped down next to me and leaned in to get a look at Dwyer.

"No, he's not dead. He's lost a lot of blood. He passed out," I explained.

"Did you call for an ambulance?" he asked.

"Yes, it's on the way. Where's the other guy?" I nodded towards Baritone man.

"He got away," he mumbled.

He went over to check for a pulse on Baritone man. He shook his head and walked back over to the entrance of the alleyway.

Soon the sirens wailed, closing in. When the paramedics arrived, the jostling to get Dwyer on the gurney woke him.

"You're going to need to come down to the station so we can discuss this." Dwyer's face was pale and his hands were clammy.

I frowned, "Do you believe me now that this isn't about drugs?"

He laughed and then winced in pain. "Do you really think now is a good time for 'I told you so'?" He smiled weakly at me.

I smiled back. "You started it."

"Don't make me laugh," he winced again.

"Should I go now, or do you want me to wait until you're...?" I didn't finish my sentence.

"Go now. My partner, Detective Stanton, can take your statement. When I'm back on my feet I'll give you a call. I'm sure I'll have some questions of my own."

They loaded Dwyer into the back of the ambulance. There was no time to say anything else. The paramedic slammed the door shut, and within seconds the ambulance shot off towards the nearest hospital. I watched the emergency vehicle until it disappeared around a corner.

There was now a multitude of police officers swarming in and around the alleyway. I barely noticed any of them. I'm not sure how long I stood staring down the street.

"My car's in the courthouse parking lot. Do you need a ride to the station?" Detective Stanton's voice brought me out of my trance.

"What? Oh, yes, if you don't mind." I shrugged. I noticed for the first time that my hands were covered in blood.

Stanton noticed too. "I have some wet wipes in my car. You can get cleaned up a bit if you want," he suggested.

I took a deep breath and realized how little I had been breathing up to this point. The air felt good in my lungs. My pulse finally began to slow. I looked around and saw my briefcase laying on the ground where I dropped it. I picked it up and followed Stanton to his car.

I cleaned as much blood off my hands as I could on our way to the station. There's really only so much wet wipes can do. Though it would have been a good time to discuss what just happened, there was an unspoken agreement to make the drive in silence. We both just needed some time to process it all.

It was well after dark by the time I finished up with Detective Stanton. We went over and over what happened. He asked every question at least three times. By the time we were finished, I couldn't recall ever feeling so exhausted. He was kind enough to call a cab to take me home. If the cabbie saw the blood stains on my clothes or arms he didn't mention it. Then again, he didn't try to talk to me at all on the ride home, so perhaps he did notice.

In the lobby of my building, Phil did a double take when he saw me enter. "Ms. Aiton, what happened? Are you okay?!" He rushed over to me.

"I'm okay. It's been a really long, horrible day. I just want to get to my apartment, take a long, hot shower, and go to bed." I didn't stop walking as I talked. I just headed straight for the elevator.

When I got to my apartment, I unlocked my door. I was greeted by an ecstatic Mort, whose whole rear end wiggled in happiness.

Becca jumped up from the couch. "I hope you don't mind if I stay here tonight. I tried calling–" she said in a rush.

She stopped midsentence when she finally noticed the blood. "What happened!?" she shrieked. "Are you hurt?"

"It's not *my* blood," I said, like that cleared everything up.

"What did you do?!" She was hysterical. She started to hyperventilate. I helped her back down on the couch.

"You need to put your head between your legs. Just focus on your breathing," I instructed her.

I spoke calming words as she tried to regain control of her panic. When she had calmed down, she looked me over again. "What happened?" she whispered.

"It's a long story, and I really, really want to get cleaned up. Let me take a shower first, and then I can explain. Okay?"

She nodded and got up from the couch. "I need a drink. Do you have any wine?"

"Check the cabinet," I said. "Have you eaten yet?"

She shook her head.

"Why don't you order a pizza? Make it a large, stuffed crust, extra cheese." I didn't wait for a response.

I locked myself in the bathroom and finally lost all sense of composure under the hot stream of water. I just stood there for twenty minutes, letting the water run over me until the warmth seeped into my weary bones. I used half a bottle of soap scrubbing my skin clean. I didn't get out until the water ran cold. I picked out my favorite pajamas and dressed slowly.

When I rejoined Becca, there was a steaming pizza sitting on the coffee table. The smell hit me and made my stomach rumble. It reminded me that I hadn't eaten all day. I grabbed a slice and sat down on the couch. Mort grumbled a bit when I had to scoot him over. He could be quite the couch hog.

"I saw Henry today." I dove right into my story.

Mort's ears perked up at his former master's name.

"What? Where?" Becca's voice was as high as her eyebrows.

"At the courthouse. I confronted him about abandoning Mort."

"Is that his blood?!" she asked, looking horrified.

"Geez, no," I nearly shouted. I set my slice of pizza down. "I just yelled at him. I didn't touch him."

"Oh, so—"

"Just let me get through it all, and then you can ask questions, okay?" My voice was harder than I meant it to be.

Becca held up her hands in a defensive position.

"Sorry," I muttered. "I've already been through this a million times with the police. It's been a long day."

Her face softened.

"After I yelled at him, he took off. I tried following him out of the courthouse, but... I lost him in the crowd. I was about to go back to your place when someone grabbed me and pulled me down an alley."

Becca gasped but didn't say anything.

"It was the two guys that followed me the other night," I said.

"The guy who broke into my place?" she interjected.

"Yeah, him and the other one. They had guns, and they

told me if I screamed they'd shoot me." My voice trembled.

"Oh, Kaly. No," Becca whispered.

"They asked me how I knew Henry," I went on.

Becca looked like she was going to say something but she stopped herself.

"I told them the truth, but they didn't believe me. I was so scared, Becca. I thought they were going to kill me. They probably would have if…."

Becca kept inching closer and closer to the edge of the couch. "If what?" Her voice was barely audible.

This whole thing felt so surreal. Like the scary stories you tell around the campfire when you're a kid. It was hard to believe it had all just happened to me. I continued with my story. "Detective Dwyer showed up."

"No way!" she shouted. "How did he know?!"

"His partner told me that they were at the courthouse testifying on a case when they saw me… come down the stairs." I picked at the cuff of my pajama pant leg. "Dwyer told his partner about the message I left him about the break-in at your place and wanted to talk to me about it. They came outside after me and saw the man grab me. They followed us into the alley, and when they saw the guns, they announced who they were. Next thing I know, bullets are flying everywhere and I'm hiding behind trash cans praying not to die."

I had to stop to catch my breath. Even after all the retellings, the story still made my stomach churn.

"Did somebody die?" Becca asked, pointing at where the blood had been on my clothes earlier.

"The guy who broke into your apartment got away. His partner wasn't so lucky. He died in the alleyway." I was absently rubbing Mort's ears as I explained.

"What about the detective?" She asked with hushed reverence.

"He was shot. I helped him until the paramedics arrived, but he was hit in the shoulder. He should be okay. His partner tried to catch the other guy but, like I said, he got away." I slouched back into the deep cushions of the couch.

Mort eyed me to see why I had stopped petting him. Becca didn't say anything for a long time. We both sat quietly, neither of us touching the pizza that was growing cold in front of us.

Finally Becca spoke. "So what do we do now?"

I shook my head. "I'm not sure. Detective Dwyer's partner said they'll run the fingerprints of the guy who died. They're hoping that will give them a lead."

There seemed to be a struggle going on in Becca's head. When she finally spoke, her grey eyes were clouded by uncertainty.

"Do you think all this has something to do with Henry?" She waved her arm around at my apartment.

"I think it has *everything* to do with Henry. And I feel like I'm even further from understanding it then I ever have been." I punched one of the pillows next to me.

"Well then, we just need to find Henry," Becca said resolutely.

"Yes, we need to find Henry."

"Any ideas on how we do that?" she asked.

I looked down at Mort and then back at her. "Actually, I think I might know a way."

CHAPTER 8

Desperate Measures

I gave the paper I was holding one final inspection. The picture of Mort's smiling face looked back at me. When I was satisfied that my flier was adequate, I placed it on the copier. I punched five and zero, then pressed start. The poster didn't take long to make. I finished it in between seeing patients. Now I just needed to put them up on my way home from work.

While the copier whirred and clunked, I went to the supply closet to stock up on everything I would need to conceal Mort in my apartment for a few days. Potty pads, dog toys, treats, and more food. I stuffed it all into the duffle bag I brought from home. I wasn't sure how Mort would like being cooped up in the apartment all weekend, but something told me he wouldn't mind too much.

I didn't know a lot about Henry, but I did know he loved his dog. If there was any way to draw him out, it would be by making him think something happened to Mort.

The lost posters were still warm when I pulled them from

the copier. I collected my things and said goodnight to Jenny on my way out. She hardly lifted her head from the gossip magazine she was reading. I was glad she was distracted. She didn't even notice the fliers or that Mort wasn't with me. I didn't want to have to stop and explain everything to her.

I visited a number of places near the clinic and put up my posters. I did the same thing close to my apartment. I didn't know where Henry was, so I wasn't sure where else to put them to ensure he would see. It felt a little weird to hope that he was still watching me.

I hid the posters when I entered the lobby. It could get complicated if I told someone in the building that my dog was missing and then they heard barking. If they saw the fliers hanging up nearby, I could just say it wasn't Mort.

Becca called out a hello from the couch when I walked in. Mort was too enraptured by the belly rub she was giving him to even notice I had arrived.

"Did you get the fliers up?" she asked.

"Yeah," I said, and handed her a copy from my bag. I dropped my duffle bag near the coffee table. "How'd it go today?" I asked.

"He must have been paper trained because he didn't have any problems using the newspaper I put down." She stopped rubbing Mort's belly, and he gave a disgruntled groan.

"Well that will certainly make this weekend easier," I laughed.

"Do you really think this will work?" she said with a raised eyebrow.

"It has to. It's the only plan I've got," I admitted.

We passed the evening on the couch watching movies and ordering takeout. I zoned out a number of times. I kept thinking about what I was going to say to Henry if he called about Mort. I wanted to know why those men were after him. Even more so, I wanted to know why they would come after *me*. I thought if I could just learn the answer to those two questions, I'd be able to figure out what to do about all of this. Because I *needed* to do something. Doing nothing hadn't worked, so now it was time for action.

The phone ringing startled me out of my daze. Becca glanced at me. She didn't have to speak. I knew what she was thinking. Henry.

"Hello?" I answered in the middle of the third ring.

"Hello. Is this Ms. Aiton?" said a voice that didn't belong to Henry.

"Who is this?" I felt my heart sink in disappointment.

"This is Detective Stanton. Dwyer wanted me to call you and give you an update."

"Oh, did you find the other man?" I asked.

"Um, no ma'am. I'm sorry, we haven't found him yet. But we did get a hit on the prints we pulled off the perp who died at the scene," he said quickly.

"Okay." I didn't know what else to say.

"The guy's got a rap sheet longer than my arm. He's a known mercenary for hire. He's worked for some pretty unsavory organizations, including those with close ties to organized crime. He's been connected with weapons trafficking, corporate espionage, money laundering, witness tampering. I mean, the list just goes on and on." He sounded a little too excited for my own comfort.

"He's a really bad guy. I think I get the picture," I croaked.

"Ms. Aiton, we're going to need you to come in. My supervisor wants me to go over a few more things. Honestly, we really just need to figure out what this kind of guy would want with you."

At least he was being honest. Though it didn't make me feel any better.

"I'd really like to know that myself, Detective. What makes you think asking me more questions will help you figure it out? I've already told you everything I know. I don't know what else you can ask that you haven't already." I tried not to sound as exasperated as I felt.

"Well that's the thing about going over things again, you never know when something might knock a new piece of information loose, maybe jog a memory. Would you be willing to come in? Or I can come to you," he offered.

I sighed. "No that's all right. I'll come in. Does it have to be now? It's pretty late."

"No, you can come by in the morning."

"Okay, I'll be there then," I replied.

"Have a good evening, ma'am." He hung up before I could return the pleasantry.

Becca was staring at me with her sunken grey eyes.

"Did you catch all that?" I asked.

My phone receiver was pretty loud. You could often hear the person on the other end of the line if you were sitting close to whoever was holding the phone. Becca nodded.

"This just keeps getting better and better," I muttered.

Becca didn't respond. I rubbed my temples and took a couple deep breaths. Mort hopped off the couch and began sniffing around the room. I knew that look. I jumped up and grabbed a potty pad out of my duffle bag. I got it down in the corner just in time. Mort did his business and then waddled into my bedroom. Apparently he was ready for bed. I couldn't blame him. I cleaned up the pad and laid a new one down just in case.

"I'm going to bed," I announced.

"Okay, goodnight," Becca mumbled.

She hadn't stayed at her apartment since the break-in. I didn't mind her staying with me. It was nice having someone else around after everything that had happened.

I got ready for bed and Mort was already snoring away when I climbed in next to him. I closed my eyes and willed myself not to open them until morning.

I don't remember what I dreamed about, but from the feeling of dread when I woke up, it wasn't good. I ate a quick breakfast, cleaned up after Mort, and took the trash with me on the way out to meet with Detective Stanton. The last thing I wanted was to be stuck in a smelly apartment all weekend.

The only surprise that came from the meeting was that Detective Dwyer was there. I was glad to see him up and about, but I was surprised he was back at work already. He still looked pale and a bit ragged. The questions were mostly the same stuff we had covered the last time. Although they did add some questions about what I knew and didn't know about various questionable organizations in the Boston area. They actually looked even more disappointed when I left then when I arrived.

I picked up some snacks on the way home. Becca, Mort, and I spent the rest of the day getting caught up on all the TV shows I had on my DVR. My phone didn't ring once. I went to bed feeling the pangs of doubt fester. I had been so sure my plan was going to work. I fell asleep to the rhythmic snoring coming from the bulldog curled up next to me.

I don't know what woke me, but it was still dark out when I opened my eyes. I stared at my clock until the red digital numbers came into focus. It was two in the morning. I lay there, staring at the ceiling, not feeling the least bit tired. Mort lifted his head, gave a little whine, and then went back to sleep.

My phone started rattling on the nightstand. I picked it up to keep it from vibrating itself off the table. My heart picked up its pace. "Hello?" I said timidly.

"The day I met you, I offered to get you something. In twenty minutes, meet me at the place where I got it. Make sure you're not followed," Henry said cryptically, then hung up.

I sat there just staring at my phone, my heart pounded in my ears. I tried to think back to the first time we met, but my nerves were doing chorus line kicks in my stomach, making it hard to focus. Then I remembered, he bumped into me and spilled my coffee. The coffee! He brought me a cup from the place just up the street from my clinic. I jumped out of bed. I shoved my feet into some shoes and woke Becca up in my rush to the door.

"What's happening? Where are you going?" she mumbled, still half asleep.

Mort came running out after me.

"Henry called. I have to go meet him." I spun around, looking for my jacket.

"You're going now? What time is it?"

"It's two, but I only have twenty minutes to get there. If I'm not back in an hour, call Detective Dwyer," I called over my shoulder and bolted out the door. I heard Mort barking as I clambered aboard the elevator.

"Is everything all right, Ms. Aiton?" Phil asked as I hurried past him in the lobby.

"Yeah." I didn't wait around for more questions.

I had to stop myself from sprinting all the way there. I kept looking over my shoulder as I went. I wasn't sure how to tell if I was being followed, so I did the best I could. I was across the street from the coffee shop and stopped to look behind me one more time. There was a car coming from the right, so I started to jog across before the car reached me. I was still six feet from the curb when I tripped and rolled to a stop right in front of the oncoming car. I heard tires screeching and muffled swearing, and I braced for impact. I didn't open my eyes until I heard a horn honking and someone shouting. "Get out of the middle of the road moron!"

I stood and stared into his blaring headlights. I can now completely empathize with deer. It took another horn honk to get me moving again. On the sidewalk, I brushed myself off and made sure I hadn't sustained any serious injuries. Everything seemed to be intact, a little banged up, but nothing broken.

I was pretty shaken up by the time I made it inside the coffee shop. I was surprised by how many people were still there at this time of night. Most of them didn't even look up from their computers when I entered. I looked around frantically for Henry but didn't see him. I glanced down at my phone, which was still clutched in my hand. It had only been eighteen minutes. I was early. I ordered a cup of coffee so I wouldn't look any more out of place than I already did.

I was just grabbing the cup from the barista when a hand grabbed my elbow. I gave an involuntary shriek before realizing it was Henry. My cheeks burned as all the coffee shop patrons glanced up from their nightly pursuits.

"Sorry," I apologized to my audience.

They all went back to their work, and Henry steered me out onto the street.

"You shouldn't sneak up on people like that," I hissed.

I was having flashbacks of being grabbed in the alleyway by the courthouse.

"I didn't mean to startle you." His cerulean blue eyes darted up and down the street.

We walked for a block, and then he pulled me up against a building so we were hidden from the light of the streetlamps. He was standing so close I found it hard to think straight. I could feel his warm breath on my face. From this proximity I had to tilt my chin up to meet his eyes.

"You know why I asked to see you." He said it as a

statement not a question.

"Yes," I answered anyway.

"What happened to Mort? Did you see who took him?" he asked.

"Why would you think someone took him?" I frowned up at him.

"I saw your posters. You said he was missing."

"As in lost, not stolen. Do you think someone would steal him?" I felt a realization tug at my gut.

"I left him with you so he would be safe." He dodged my question.

"You're afraid someone would steal him. That means you know he's worth stealing. Why? Start explaining right now. You need to tell me what is going on. I can't take it anymore!" I demanded.

"Where was he taken from, your apartment or the clinic?" He was still ignoring my questions.

"I'm not answering any more of your questions until you answer mine." I crossed my arms over my chest.

He looked around again and stepped closer. He pressed both hands against the building, one arm on either side of me so that I was pinned in place. "He has something that can either help or harm everyone on this planet, so you need to tell me right now where and when he was taken." His face was inches from mine. His eyes kept falling to my lips. It was so distracting.

I tried to think. How could a dog have something like that? I tried to process what he said, but I couldn't focus. All I felt was heat, like I was standing too close to a raging fire and I couldn't move away.

"I… he… er, I mean, isn't, wasn't taken. Yeah, he's not taken. Wasn't taken," I stammered. "What is wrong with you?"

That last part I directed at myself.

"Wait, he wasn't taken? So, what, he ran away? He's just lost?" He let go of the building so he could grab my arms instead.

"No, he's not lost. He's at my apartment," I said with a guilty smile.

"WHAT?!"

"I… I just wanted, no, *needed* to see you. So I made those posters 'cause it was the only way I could think of to get you to talk to me. And I was right 'cause it worked." I was rambling and defensive at the same time. It's a talent of mine.

He closed his eyes. I couldn't tell if he was trying to remain calm or if he was just relieved. He was still gripping my arms tightly, so I was inclined to think it was the former. I was surprised when he opened his eyes and I saw it was the latter. His look of relief made my muscles relax. Well, a little anyways.

"So Mort's okay? He's safe?" he persisted.

I nodded.

"And you did all this just to see me?" A smile played on his lips.

"Well not like that." I felt my face burn. "I need to know what's going on. First the break-ins, then the park stalking and dog frisking, and I was grabbed in the alleyway and then the police shootout. The detectives said the guy who grabbed me was a really bad man. I need to know what's going on." It all came out in a rush.

"Hold on, slow down. Who grabbed you? And there was a police shootout!?"

"Yes, at the courthouse that day. I ran out to catch you, but someone caught me. Two men with guns. Thankfully the detective I've been talking to about the break-ins saw it happen and came to help me. They all started shooting. One of the guys that grabbed me died. They said he's some big, bad mercenary. And I want to know why in the world a guy like that would be after me!" I was shouting now.

He put his fingers to my lips to quiet me. I made some weird squeaking noise I still have nightmares about.

"Are you all right. Did they hurt you?" His voice was heavy with guilt and concern.

I felt his eyes slowly assess me from head to foot. "No, they didn't hurt me. They shot the detective, but it hit him in the shoulder and he'll survive," I said quietly.

I couldn't help but notice that his hand was still on my chin.

"I'm sorry I dragged you into all this," he said softly.

"That's okay." My heart spoke out loud while my brain silently screamed, "No it's not, moron. We almost died!"

"You're right. You deserve an explanation. But we can't stay here. It could take a while." His voice was husky.

"Okay," my heart said again. My brain just rolled its eyes and gave up. It knows when it's in a battle it can't win.

"Come on." He took my hand. "I know somewhere we can go, and then I promise to answer all of your questions as best I can."

CHAPTER 9
Meteors and Artificial Intelligence

We walked for nearly twenty minutes, up one street, down another, doubling back and abruptly stopping. The night was cool, and I could smell rain in the air. Henry obviously knew what he was doing. If there had been anyone following us, we would have seen them.

"Who are you?" I asked for the third time that night.

"I'll explain everything once I know it's safe to talk." He smiled reassuringly.

We ended up on a little bench looking out over Boston Harbor. There was no one else around at this time of night. The boats bobbed out on the water, their lights hovering above the waves like ghosts in the mist. The waves lapped gently against the concrete shoreline a few yards from where we sat. I didn't notice the little black box until Henry was swiping it close to the front of my jacket, spending extra time around the pocket area.

"What are you doing?" I yelped. I moved farther away from him on the wooden bench. The paint was once green, but most of it was now peeled off or washed out by the sun.

"I have to make sure they didn't plant anything on you," he explained. He finished moving the box around my body. His eyes never left the little green light that blazed steadily from the small antennae.

"Why would they do that?" I shouldn't have been so surprised.

"Let me start at the beginning and tell you the whole story. If you still have questions I can answer them when I'm finished, okay?" he said.

I nodded mutely.

He leaned back on the bench and tracked a boat with his eyes. The small ship slid silently by us, the skipper careful not to kick up too much of a wake.

Henry took a deep breath. "In the early morning hours of February 8th, 1969 a meteorite fell to earth over Chihuahua, a state in Mexico. The giant ball of fire was roughly the size of a car and could be seen for hundreds of miles. On its descent, it broke apart into thousands of pieces that were scattered over an immense region in Northern Mexico."

He ignored my quizzical look and continued his story.

"If you remember, 1969 was during the height of the space craze, so there was a lot of excitement about the meteor. Planetary scientists from around the globe went to collect samples, eager for what it might teach them. Among those who went to search for pieces was an eccentric millionaire named Mortimer Reynolds."

I gave him a look when he mentioned the rich guy's name.

Henry laughed. "Yes, I named my dog after an eccentric millionaire. Their personalities were strikingly similar."

I couldn't help but laugh as I pictured Mort and some wealthy geezer in smoking jackets sitting in a cozy library somewhere, snoring in front of a blazing fire.

Henry continued his story, breaking me out of my daydream. "Mortimer found a rather large chunk of the meteor. It was about a foot-and-a-half at its widest and shaped a bit like a football."

Henry held out his hands to estimate the size of the meteor.

"But instead of sharing his significant-sized find with the scientific community, he hid it away in his study. It remained undetected until Mortimer died a few years ago."

I couldn't take it anymore, I had to interrupt. "What does this have to do with you?"

Henry gave me an impatient look. "Mortimer was my grandfather. My father died shortly after I was born, so I inherited my grandfather's estate."

"Oh," I said with an embarrassed smile. "So you found the meteor?"

Henry nodded. "I was cleaning out his study, and I saw it. I had studied other pieces of the Allende meteorite during my undergrad work, so I had a feeling it was from the same meteor."

He held up a hand to quiet me when he noticed I was about to interrupt again. "It's made of a rather distinctive material," he explained. "But still, when I saw it, I couldn't believe how large it was! Most meteor fragments aren't that big so, this was a rare find. The scientist in me couldn't rest until I took it in to be analyzed."

I tried to stifle a yawn but wasn't successful.

Henry noticed and smiled weakly. "Sorry, I'll skip over the analysis process. Long story short, we found something in the center of the meteor chunk," Henry said, his eyes flashing.

"You found something?" I said slowly.

"Yes. But to get to it we would have to drill into the meteor. There was a lot of arguing over whether we should cut into it or not. The two schools of thought on the matter–" He stopped when he caught me yawn again.

He sighed. "We ended up cutting the meteor open and retrieving what was inside."

This caught my interest. "What was it?"

"It was a small piece of matter like nothing anyone had ever seen before. It was a perfect rectangle. No bigger than the width and length of your pinky."

He plucked up my littlest finger and held it up for me to examine for comparison. I felt a flutter in my stomach.

"It was transparent, with a tint of purple. And whatever material it was made from was completely indestructible. We studied it for days without being able to glean anything from it."

I frowned. "Did you ever figure out what it was?"

His excitement grew with each word. "It happened by accident one day. A lab tech set her cell phone down next to it."

"Her cell phone?" I said.

He nodded. "And then the strangest thing happened." He stopped, he knew he had me hooked and waited for me to beg him to continue.

"Well? What happened?!" I obliged.

"She got a text message," he said with a mischievous grin.

"A text message!? That isn't even remotely strange!" I yelled.

The glint was still in his eye. "It was from the space object."

I don't think I've ever scoffed so hard in my life as I did just then.

Henry held up his hands. "The tech didn't believe it either at first. She thought it was one of her coworkers trying to prank her. She played along for a while, but the more they texted, the more she realized she was talking to someone who wasn't from our planet."

I laughed in his face. "So what, the space object is really an alien?"

"No, but it was an AI program *created* by an intelligent life form that is not from this world," he answered with all seriousness.

"AI?" I asked.

"Artificial intelligence. The program learned and adapted to the information it collected. Rather quickly I might add. It taught itself how to speak our language. Then it told us that its creators sent it out to search for other intelligent races in the universe."

I just stared at him for a moment. "You're crazy," I said when I couldn't think of anything else to say.

"I know it sounds like it, but I'm telling the truth."

"For argument's sake, say I believe you, which I don't, but we'll pretend for a moment that I do. Why are there people after you, and now me?" I asked.

"Those men work for a company called Pastern Inc. The company works in applied sciences and are always looking for new scientific breakthroughs. They are in it solely for the money and have no qualms about advancing their research without any regard for ethical considerations. They heard about our discovery and they want it for themselves. They think it will advance science, and their pocketbooks, by hundreds if not thousands of years and billions of dollars," Henry explained.

I thought about it for a moment. In all the scenarios that had gone through my head, this wasn't even close to one of them. "So wait a minute." Realization struck me. "They think you have or had the AI program and that you gave it to me?"

"Yes."

"Why would they think that?" I accused.

"Because they've looked everywhere else. I took her out of the lab when I learned Pastern was interested. After hearing about the shady things that always seemed to happen whenever they were involved, I didn't want them to get their hands on her. I knew how dangerous that could be. So I hid her."

"You keep saying her?" I squinted at him. "Do you mean the lab tech with the cell phone?"

"No, the AI. I call her a woman because, the name she

calls herself… it's a girl's name."

I could see the hint of blush on his cheeks even in the darkness of the early-morning hour.

"The space program named itself?" My head was starting to hurt.

His smile was awkward. "Yes, her name… actually she chose, that is, I mean… she picked the name Kaly."

His rushed revelation was like a punch in the chin.

***

It reminded me of the time when I was nine and fell at the gas station. I had my hands in my pockets when I tripped over a tiny bump on the island where the pumps sat. I fell off the curb like a tree falls in the forest, quietly and without even the slightest wiggle of self-preservation. I landed face first on my chin, effectively breaking my jaw, which required having my teeth wired shut for six weeks.

***

That situation felt very similar to this one. Henry's confession that the AI shared my name was like that same jarring shock to my system.

When I fell at the gas station, at first I didn't realize what had happened. But then alarm bells went off. I knew something odd was going on but I couldn't quite put my finger on it. Later on I would be puking my guts out from the pain. But for a moment, I lay in stunned silence.

Just as I now sat in stunned silence and the alarm bells were going off. I just prayed Henry's admission wouldn't have me puking my guts out later.

"You named her after me?" I asked weakly.

"No, she chose the name herself before I ever met you. Then when I ran into you in front of your clinic and you told me your name, I got the crazy idea to hide her with you. I *thought* you would be far enough removed from me that when I hid her and Mort with you, they would never suspect you. I guessed wrong."

"And you were just going to leave Mort and her, er, it with me forever?" I said.

"No, I'm working on a plan to keep her safe permanently, but I thought they would be okay with you until I got everything worked out." He stared down at a spot of gum stuck to the sidewalk near his feet.

"So let me see if I've got all this straight? A program created by aliens, rode a meteor down to earth looking for intelligent life. The program taught itself how to speak English and text message and then named itself Kaly. Now evil scientists, who don't mind hiring mercenaries, are trying to steal it from you. But they can't find it because you hid it and your dog with a perfect stranger because she had the same name as your alien robot."

"Well gee, when you say it like that, it sounds a bit ridiculous." Henry's sarcasm was palpable.

"Is that why that guy frisked Mort the other day?" I blurted out.

"He was probably looking for the program. They're

nothing if not thorough. They've searched everywhere else, so I'm not surprised they searched him too," Henry answered.

"Why didn't they find it?" I asked.

"I'm surprised they didn't. It's right there in his collar," he said.

My heart dropped. "I took his collar off to give him a bath, I forgot to put it back on. He wasn't wearing it."

Henry laughed. "Congratulations, you single-handedly outsmarted some of the toughest goons in the business!"

I just shook my head. "This doesn't mean I believe you by the way."

He shrugged. "I don't blame you, but I can prove it."

My eyes flew to his.

"You've got the program wherever you left Mort's collar. Just put it near a computer or cell phone. Kaly can tell you herself that everything I've said is true," he said.

It was weird hearing him say my name while talking about some kind of program. But he was right. If he was lying, all I had to do was go home and put Mort's collar near my phone. When nothing happened, I could just write this guy off as a nut job and vow never to talk to him again.

But what if he was telling the truth?

He led the way back toward the coffee shop. He didn't say anything. He just let me ruminate over everything we had discussed.

We were still a few blocks from the shop when Nasal man jumped out of the shadows in front of us and pointed a gun at Henry's head. "Where is it Henry?" His voice sounded even more petulant than it had the last time.

I gasped so loudly that I drew Nasal man's glare away from Henry. In that split second, Henry lunged for the gun. They struggled to the ground in their attempt to control the firearm. I reached instinctively in my pocket and found my trusty can of pepper spray. It took me a moment to pull it free, and I flipped the safety release. I aimed it at the bad guy's eyes. A rush coursed through me. I felt nothing short of heroic as I plunged the trigger of the spray.

My adrenalin was short lived. It was followed immediately by a burning agony in my eyes. I contemplated what went wrong as I crumpled to the ground in a heap. My eyes felt as though they were on fire, tears poured freely from my ducts. Only then did I realize that I must have had the nozzle facing the wrong direction.

In my self-induced suffering, I heard a distinct thud and the familiar sound of a body falling to the pavement. Then I heard the scraping sound of the can and the hiss of more spray being released. I tried to peer through the blur of tears to see what was going on. I felt someone move close to me and take something out of my pocket.

"Yes, I need to report an attempted mugging." It was Henry. He was on the phone, my phone.

When he finished the call he slipped the phone back in my pocket and leaned near my ear. "They'll be here soon. Tell them you sprayed him with the pepper spray and then knocked him out with the butt of the gun. If they ask about your eyes, tell them you got some of the spray on your hands and rubbed them."

My vision was only clear enough to make out a wavy blob where he stood. "Are you leaving?!" I could hear the panic in my own voice.

"You can't tell the police about Kaly. They have to make reports and tell supervisors. There's too much of a chance the information will leak. It could be very dangerous if more people found out about it."

I didn't answer. I just sat on the sidewalk nursing my watering eyeballs. I wasn't ready to make any promises just yet. I wanted a bit more time to think before I committed to anything.

"We'll talk again soon. I'll find you," he whispered, and his dark shadow rolled away.

I was left with my pain and the very real possibility that Henry was a crazy loon. But still, I couldn't help but wonder, if I was so sure Henry's story was completely insane why was I so anxious to get home and put his "proof" to the test?

CHAPTER 10
Surreal Conversations

"You're a complete idiot, you know that?" I said to myself for the fifth time in the last half an hour.

I stared at my phone, debating whether I should call Detective Dwyer and confess everything I withheld from the police. A few hours ago, a kind patrolman arrived shortly after Henry left and took Nasal man into custody. I told the patrolman it was an attempted mugging. I obediently fed him the story Henry instructed me to give. The whole time I had a pit in my stomach. I had never lied to a police officer before.

"You're such a moron." This time I gave my forehead a good slap to emphasize my point.

I don't know what possessed me to lie the way I did. Whatever it was, it was still in possession of my common sense because here I sat staring at my computer, waiting for something to happen. I pulled the small purple disk out of Mort's collar as soon as Becca left to go back to her apartment. I told her the police had Nasal man in custody, which was true. I just conveniently left out the part about my run-in with Henry and all the stuff about aliens and meteors. She was so relieved that the bad guy had been caught, she didn't stick around to ask many more questions. I was grateful for that.

I moved the disk a little closer to my new computer, as though that would help. I stared at the blank screen for half an hour with nothing to show for it. Maybe artificial intelligence programs didn't know how to speak Microsoft Word? I didn't know what the proper procedure was for contacting alien technology, so I opened the first thing I knew I could type into: a Word document. The cursor blinked morosely at me as I waited. I argued with myself once more about picking up my phone to call Detective Dwyer. Then I pleaded with myself to wait just a little while longer.

It was not my finest moment. The internal battle raged. Then I came up with a bargain. Yes, with myself. I would try typing something, and if I didn't get a response within five minutes, I would call Detective Dwyer and tell him everything. With an illogical instinct, I turned to look over my shoulder, as though someone may have snuck into my otherwise empty apartment to watch me make a fool of myself. With a final breath, I tapped out the first thing that popped into my head.

Hello? Kaly, are you there?

I had to erase a couple letters that I added by accident from the tremble in my fingers. I didn't let out my breath, I just held it. I listened to the blood pounding louder and louder in my ears the longer my lungs went without oxygen. Then I fell out of my chair. Not because I passed out, but because there on my computer screen, in my half-hour-old Word document, came a response!

Henry? Is that you?

I screeched and hurtled towards the floor. I knocked over the desk lamp on my spastic journey down.

Mort snorted himself awake and lifted his head to investigate from the couch where he was sleeping. He eyed me and then the desk lamp on the floor and then me again. Deciding it wasn't worth the effort, he circled once and laid back down to resume his nap.

My heart pounded as I lay on the hardwood floor. Was I expecting an answer? Was I *not* expecting an answer? Nothing made sense. I was so confused. When lying prone on the floor didn't solve anything, I lifted a hand to grasp the edge of my writing desk. I hauled myself back into my seat and reread those four little words that changed everything.

This isn't Henry, I typed slowly.

I had no idea what to type next. What do you say to the program created by aliens that gets sent to your planet to make contact with other intelligent life? We come in peace? That seemed ludicrous. No, scratch that, everything seemed ludicrous. I didn't know what to do, so I waited.

How do you know my name? she wrote.

Finally! A question I could answer! I nearly shoved the keyboard off the desk in my rush to answer.

Henry told me. He told me about you.

I stood and awaited her response. Sitting still took too much effort.

Where is he? I want to talk to him.

He's not here, I typed.

Where is he?

I don't know, I answered truthfully.

Why do you have my operating shell? She seemed to be getting an attitude.

Is it possible for programs to have attitude?

Henry gave me your shell for safekeeping. He was being followed and needed a safe place to hide you, I replied.

Who are you? How do I know I'm in a safe place right now? There is no information on this machine.

It was like I could hear her being huffy through the computer screen.

My name is Kaly, too. This computer is new. That's why there's nothing on it.

I felt a little ridiculous explaining myself to something that wasn't much more than a computer program.

Well, Kaly too, how do I know you won't try to use me for nefarious purposes? Henry has warned me there are many beings on your planet who would do so.

This question stumped me. How do you convince someone, in this case an AI, that your intentions are honorable? Were my intentions honorable? Would I even know how to use her for nefarious purposes?

I wouldn't even know how to use you for evil. I don't really understand what it is you do, I responded.

I have a wealth of information. Our sciences are far

advanced from the primitive work currently being done on your planet. Henry seemed to think our biological compounds would be of the most interest. He claims some would use them to make horrible weapons. Why they would do this to members of their own species is beyond my comprehension.

I blew out a long breath as I contemplated this. *Well first of all, if you're not sure you can trust someone, you really shouldn't be telling them stuff like that. And second, I'm a doctor, so I'm more interested in healing than I am in harming,* I typed.

This was a test earthborn, to see how you would respond. I have found your answer satisfactory and will continue to communicate with you. My creators were also healers and were very interested in learning from other species in the hopes of advancing medical sciences. It was their belief that this could be beneficial to both races.

This really got the ole neurons firing in my brain. If we could communicate with an alien race as progressive as this one, medicine could advance exponentially. My mind raced with all the possibilities. *Well, I'm not a human doctor, I'm an animal doctor, but I think such a program would be highly beneficial,* I answered.

There was a long pause. I watched the cursor expectantly, but nothing happened.

Are you still there? I asked.

You are a doctor to animals?

Yes.

Are animals intelligent on your planet? Does your world have more than one sentient species? Henry and the other *scientist I spoke with made it seem like there was only one.*

Now it was my turn to hesitate. *Well, they aren't as intelligent as we are, no.*

And yet you have doctors for them?

Yes.

I am having a difficult time reconciling the cultural norms of your planet. Please help me comprehend. You have no moral concerns with using biological weapons on those of your own species, but you value lower species enough to provide doctors for them?

I blinked a few times. I hadn't thought of it in such terms before. Now that she mentioned it, it did seem rather contradictory. *Well not all of us are okay with biological weapons.* It was the only response I could come up with.

I cannot say that assists me in reconciling the matter. The fact that your species has such polar opposite tendencies baffles my programing.

If it makes it any easier for you, it baffles my programing too, I quipped.

Ah yes, that was an attempt at what you call "humor" was it not? Henry taught me about that. Unfortunately my parameters do not allow me to appreciate it the way you do. So you need not attempt your jokes. I do not wish to offend you by not offering an appropriate response.

Ouch. I've had people tell me my jokes were bad, but somehow this felt worse. *Okay. No more jokes. Got it,* I typed.

I couldn't believe I was getting so offended by a computer program. I shook my head to help clear my thoughts and tried to figure out what to do next. *I don't know what to do now,* I finally wrote.

The last time I communicated with Henry, he told me he was working on recruiting other scientists who would want to use the connection to my creators for beneficial purposes. So it appears all you have to do now is keep me safe until he is ready.

Oh, gee, is that all I have to do? I knew she wouldn't pick up on my sarcasm but I couldn't resist.

Yes.

I rolled my eyes. *Well, they've already searched my home and the place I work, and they haven't found you, so I would assume you're safe for the time being.*

There is a saying on the planet where I was created. It's about assuming things, she replied.

My jaw dropped. What were the odds they had a saying similar to the earth axiom? *What do they say?* In my head, these typed words were whispered.

That you shouldn't assume things, she replied.

I snorted. *Clever,* I wrote. I couldn't tell you what spurred on my need to be sarcastic to a computer. Perhaps it was just a way to cope with the abnormality of it all. Humor had always been my default coping mechanism. It was the only way I knew how to deal with my accident-prone nature. I would make jokes or play up the hilarity of the unfortunate circumstance I often found myself in.

Like the time some friends and I were choreographing a sword fight sequence for a play. We were using brooms for swords since that was all we had on hand. It was going exceptionally well. I was pleased with my maneuvering, and the scene was nearly finished. Then, the maladroit in me reared its ugly head.

Next thing I know, I missed my mark and my friend sliced open my arm with the jagged hook on the end of his broom. It's amazing how much damage a decrepit old piece of plastic can do. I should have gone to the hospital for stitches, but honestly, how can you look a doctor in the eye and tell them you sliced your arm open on a broom?

Besides, what's a scar or two among friends right? I played up the absurdity of the injury whenever anyone asked about the scar. They laughed. I laughed. It was how I coped.

⁕

So it wasn't surprising that I was using humor to deflect the craziness. It was just too bad I was communicating with something that didn't understand humor. I would just have to laugh for the both of us.

I think it would be safest to keep me hidden until Henry comes back for me, she instructed.

Okay. What else could I do? I wasn't about to sit there and argue with an alien program. *Well, goodbye then, Kaly. It was nice communicating with you,* I typed, unsure of how to end a conversation like this.

It was pleasant conversing with you as well, Kaly too.

I hesitated for a moment and then slipped the disk back into Mort's collar. No sooner had I pulled it away from the screen then the whole document went white. All the words that were there only a moment ago were suddenly gone. I checked the autosave file. Even that was cleared. There was nothing left of the conversation. I was about to put the disk next to my computer once more just to prove that I didn't imagine the whole thing, when Mort started growling.

Next came a knock at my door. Mort jumped off the couch and tottered towards the door, barking as he went. When I got to the door, I reached down and snapped the collar around his neck. I had to scoot him over so I could get in a good position to look through my peephole. My heart dropped when I saw a uniformed police officer. Mort was still barking and trying to get at whoever was on the other side. I held him back and opened the door a few inches.

The officer eyed Mort suspiciously. Without taking his eyes off him he spoke. "I'm going to need you to restrain your dog while I'm here, ma'am."

"Sure," I said. "Just let me grab his leash."

After I hooked the leash onto Mort's collar, the police officer relaxed a little.

"Just be sure to keep him away from me. If he comes at me, I will have to assume it's to attack me, and I will take appropriate precautions," he warned.

I would have laughed at that but I could see the officer was dead serious, so I just nodded.

"I am here with a warrant to search your premises," he continued.

"Excuse me?" I stammered.

"You were in an altercation early this morning with a

man by the name of Barlow Pepperton," he stated, reading from the warrant in his hand.

"Um, a man tried to mug me this morning, but I don't know his name," I said weakly.

"Pepperton is claiming that it is the other way around, and that you mugged him."

"He what?!" I shouted.

Mort started barking. The police officer placed a hand on his gun. I tightened my grip on Mort's leash and pulled him back a couple of feet.

"Mr. Pepperton states that you approached him with a gun and demanded he hand over a proprietary computer disk that he was carrying. When he refused to give it to you, you sprayed him with mace and knocked him out. Then while he was unconscious, you stole said disk." The officer was reading from the papers he was holding.

He held the warrant out for me to inspect.

"You have got to be kidding!" I exclaimed. "So he's claiming that I robbed him and then called the police on myself?!"

The officer didn't say anything. I shook my head and stared at the warrant. I could not believe this was happening.

"And you believe him?!" My voice was easily two octaves higher than normal.

"Ma'am, I'm just here to execute this warrant. I think it would be best if you waited outside with your dog," he said, eyeing Mort. "This is Officer Stanley and Officer O'Riley. They'll be helping me execute this warrant. We will be removing anything that resembles a computer disk. You are free to contact an attorney at this time, should you choose to do so."

And with that, they began their search. Starting with my pockets. They let me turn them inside out and observed me from a healthy distance, a few feet outside the reach of Mort's leash. Clearly they thought this search was bogus; they weren't putting much effort into it. I decided it was probably just best to leave them to it, and I informed them I would be taking Mort for a walk.

"You will need to be available for questioning should our search turn up anything." The officer said as he rummaged through my desk.

"Just grab one of my cards there on my desk. It's got my cell phone number on it. I'm more than happy to answer any questions. Mr. Pepperton is a flat-out liar, and I will gladly put my word against his any day of the week," I spat.

If his rap sheet was anything like his partner's, I wasn't too worried about whose word they would believe in this situation. When the officer didn't add anything, I tugged Mort's leash and we went out into the hall. If you had asked me a couple of months ago whether I would ever consider leaving perfect strangers alone to search my apartment, I would have called you crazy. But after everything that had happened, I didn't give it a second thought.

Mort and I made our way out of my building as if it were any other day. We ignored the questions from the security guard in the lobby and walked out into the sunshine. The day was bright and clear. It was hard to believe my life could be so completely upside-down when the weather was so lovely.

I just needed to pretend everything was normal for a little while, just a little ho-hum in the midst of chaos. We pushed our way out the door and as we turned to walk up the street, I prayed we could make it to the park and back without incident.

CHAPTER 11
Aliens and Abduction

The police were getting ready to leave when Mort and I got back. I held the leash taunt, but Mort just snorted with casual indifference at the officers. He tugged me in the direction of the couch. Two officers left without much more than a goodbye, but Officer O'Riley hung back. He looked like he wanted to say something.

"So what happens now?" I asked him, to try to get him talking.

"If anything we collected matches the description of the item Mr. Pepperton claims you took, we'll have enough evidence to file charges. You'll have a warrant issued for your arrest." O'Riley paused. He shifted uncomfortably, looked out into the empty hallway and then back at me. "Look ma'am, I could get into trouble telling you this but…. You seem like a nice lady, and you help take care of sick animals. My little sister wants to be a vet when she grows up."

I smiled politely and nodded. I stayed quiet. I hoped it would keep him talking.

"It seems you've made a very powerful enemy, Ms. Aiton," he continued. "Whoever had this warrant issued has to have a lot of pull to have it executed so quickly. Honestly, in my twelve years on the force, I've never seen it happen so fast."

This made my head swim. My heartbeat picked up its pace. I chewed on my tongue while I tried to process this bit of information.

O'Riley continued in my silence. "I don't know whether you took whatever it is we were looking for, but if you did, I suggest you return it as quickly as possible. I can't help but think your own safety may be at stake here, and I'd hate to see anything happen to you."

The last part sounded like a threat. Then again, I was finding it difficult to distinguish appropriate paranoia from ridiculous paranoia lately. "I didn't take anything, Officer. Mr. Pepperton accosted me, not the other way around," I stated, trying to keep my voice level.

O'Riley paused to watch me for a moment and then nodded his head. "That's the thought at the station, Ms. Aiton. It could just be a retaliatory accusation cooked up by Mr. Pepperton's attorney. He's a pretty high-powered lawyer. I wouldn't put it past him to have a few of those tricks up his sleeve. Sorry to have intruded. It was nothin' personal. We were just doing our job."

O'Riley tipped his head towards me and then left my apartment without another word. I closed the door quietly and locked it. Leaning back against it, I took a couple deep breaths. I just wanted to crawl back into bed and pretend this had all been a bad dream. But I was too rattled to sleep, so I grabbed my cell phone off the kitchen table where I left it. I settled down on the couch next to Mort and punched in my work number.

"Aiton's Animal Clinic, this is Jenny. How may I assist you?" She answered on the third ring.

"Hey, it's me. I was just calling to remind you that I won't be in today," I said.

"Oh hi, Kaly. Yes, I remember. When do you think you'll be back?"

"Hopefully tomorrow. I just… I'm just not feeling too great right now. So I thought I would take the day and see how it goes," I answered truthfully.

"Okay, just let me know as soon as you can if you won't be here tomorrow. Feel better," she said in her airy voice and then hung up.

I dropped my phone on the couch, narrowly missing Mort's wrinkled head. With a few commands of my remote, I found a movie I loved that had just started. I was so immersed in the action near the end of the movie that I almost missed the buzz of my phone. I picked it up and noticed I had a new text message. I opened it and gasped when I read it.

Kaly too, I wanted to let you know. I communicated with Henry, and he says he is nearly ready to come for me.

I leaned down close to Mort's collar. I wasn't sure how close I would need to be to respond.

That sounds like good news. Did he say he would be coming here to get you? To my apartment I mean.

He told me that he is working on an extraction plan, and he will contact you once everything is in place, Virtual Kaly replied.

How were you able to communicate with him? I asked, when I couldn't think of anything else to say.

This device you have me next to can connect to many other devices. I simply found the one I knew he would use and hailed him there, she explained.

Now I was *really* out of things to say. She didn't seem to have anything else to add either. After half an hour of silence, I stopped checking the phone and ordered dinner. There was a deli nearby that made a killer sub sandwich. I ordered two so it would cost enough to allow delivery, and I was soon munching on the delicious sub. The other one was stored safely in my fridge for later.

After dinner I finally felt the pull of fatigue. I got ready for bed and burrowed down under my covers, grateful I had splurged and gotten the nine-hundred thread count Egyptian cotton sheets. Everything seemed so much better when I was ensconced in my luxuriously soft bed. I don't remember falling asleep, but I remember waking up.

My eyes flew open when I felt a hand clamp over my mouth. I blinked and squinted in my darkened room and Pepperton came into focus, standing over me. Up until that point, I thought the shootout in the alleyway was the scariest thing I would ever encounter. But this was worse, so much worse.

I could smell a slight antiseptic scent on his fingers. It mixed with his pungent B.O. He smiled with only half of his mouth. There was a crazed tint to his gaze. He leaned in until I could feel his breath on my face. I had to shift my head to breathe. His hand was blocking the side of my nose that still worked.

A few years back, I was on vacation with some friends. We spent a week in a paradise known as Puerto Rico. We spent a day on a small island just east of P.R.

The island of Culebra is a gorgeous spot with some amazing beaches and opportunities for killer snorkeling. Our day was winding down as the pink-orange sun sank lazily in the west. I was standing knee-deep in the salty waters, letting the waves push and pull me.

Then suddenly, through uncanny timing mixed with my bad luck, the undertow sucked my feet out from under me just as the crest of a wave crashed into the top half of my body. I was slammed head first into the powder white sands, which don't feel nearly as soft when you hit them full force with your face.

The flash of pain was so intense I gasped and in the process sucked in a mouth full of seawater. I tried to stand but was still dizzy from the blow, and the waves were relentless in their tugging towards the ocean floor.

It was in this panicked state that I was scooped up into the muscular arms of a handsome rescuer. He looked like Tarzan, complete with tanned, sculpted muscles, chiseled features, and long brown dreadlocks. He carried me gallantly from the ocean and laid me gently on the beach.

I don't know of many girls who *don't* dream of being rescued by a smoking-hot guy, but the only thing I was feeling was mortification. There was nothing romantic about that rescue. I was a sputtering, bloody (literally) mess. My nose was swollen to three times its original size and I was working on two black eyes to boot. Nothing like the dainty, beautiful damsels of the fairy tales.

Aside from the lingering sense of embarrassment, I was also left with a nose that never quite healed properly. I never went to a doctor to get it fixed, so only one side of my nose now worked.

After getting said nostril clear of my assailant's hand, he finally spoke. "I'm going to remove my hand, but if you scream, I will shoot you." To emphasize his point, he pulled a small black pistol out of his waistband and waved it at me with his free hand. I nodded under his painful grip on my face. He removed his hand slowly, watching me through lowered lids.

I glanced around and noticed an absence that made my panic increase. "Where's my dog?" I demanded.

"I tranq'ed him and stuffed him in the closet. Couldn't have 'im gettin' in the way. That's one vicious dog you've got." He showed me the fresh puncture wounds on his arm.

I felt a flash of relief and a bit of pride that Mort had tried to protect me. "Do you often carry around a tranquilizer?"

My voice dripped with vitriol.

"It *was* for *you* until your dog attacked me." Pepperton shrugged.

"Are you going to kill me?" I blurted out.

"That depends," he said, and when I stayed quiet he continued. "You didn't tell the police what's really going on. That may have just saved your life. You give me what I need and keep your mouth shut, and you may just get out of this alive."

I found it hard to believe him. Still I nodded, what else could I do?

"Henry gave you something, didn't he? A small transparent disk? Give it to me, and I'll leave right now and you'll never see me again." He spoke so earnestly.

I wanted desperately to give in. I just wanted this all over with, but I knew what would happen once he had that disk. I knew I had to get us out of this apartment if I had any hope of staying alive long enough to see tomorrow.

"It's not here," I said.

He didn't look like he bought what I was selling. He opened his mouth to speak but I cut him off.

"You searched my place yourself, didn't you." It wasn't a question. "And you didn't find it because it's not here."

I thought half-truths would be more believable then full-on lies.

"Tell me where it is then," he growled.

I shook my head. I saw the anger rise to his nearly black eyes. His hand twitched, and he gripped his gun tighter. I had to swallow a couple times before I could speak past the lump in my throat. "If I tell you where it is, there's nothing stopping you from killing me," I explained. "So I'll take you there, and then you let me go. Everyone gets what they want."

He thought it over for a moment. I thought for sure he was going to refuse. "Fine, let's go," he muttered.

He waved his gun towards the door. I tried to climb out of bed, but the sheets were still tangled with my legs. I hadn't gone two steps when I crashed to the floor. Pepperton swore behind clenched teeth. I scrambled to disengage myself from the bedding. He grabbed me to haul me to my feet and shoved me towards the bedroom door. I glanced at the closet as we walked by.

I quickly put on a pair of shoes, not bothering to tie the laces. As I reached for my coat, Pepperton intercepted me. He ran his hands over the pockets and pulled out my can of mace.

"Wouldn't want you tryin' nuthin' foolish," he sneered.

He slipped the mace into his pocket and shoved the empty coat into my hands. I yanked my arms into my coat so hard I heard a ripping noise. Before I could investigate where the rip occurred, Pepperton nudged me out the door.

"Do you have a car?" I asked.

He gave me a suspicious look.

"We're going to need a car to get there," I stated.

He grunted and pushed me into the hall. Not bothering to lock my door, he wrestled me down the hall and onto the elevator. I pulled my arm out of his grip and knocked into him every chance I got. I needed him focused on me and not where we were going.

I had a destination in mind, but I was sure he would resist if I gave him too much time to think about it. We walked past Dean in the lobby. The morning security guard yawned and barely looked up from his morning paper. I made a mental note to have him fired later. If there was a later.

We exited onto the sidewalk just as the first rays of sun shot over the horizon. It peeked through the spaces between the buildings and caught my gaze every so often, making me squint. Pepperton tried to keep a tight grip on my arm while discretely keeping the gun pressed against my rib cage. I tugged my arm free a couple times just to hold his concentration. He led me to an old, grey Buick parked half a block up the street.

"You drive. And you try anything crazy, I will shoot you," he snarled.

He waited until I was seated behind the steering wheel before he climbed into the seat behind me. I took my time with the seatbelt and adjusting the mirror. I could feel the gun pointed at me even though I could no longer see it. I continued to fiddle with the mirrors as we drove. I made sure to keep my hands moving.

I watched him through the rearview mirror. I wanted his eyes on me. I took an indirect route so it took us nearly forty minutes to get to our destination. By the time we got there, we had taken so many unnecessary turns, even I felt a bit unsure about where we were going.

I pulled the Buick to an abrupt halt and got out before Pepperton could stop me. I could hardly believe my luck. We had arrived.

CHAPTER 12
Maladroit Ever After

He jumped out quickly, pulling me to him so the gun was concealed between us. For the first time, Pepperton looked around to see where we were. He swore under his breath when he realized we were parked in front of Terminal A of Boston Logan Airport.

"Hurry up and unload, and then move your cars," a voice shouted.

We both turned in the direction of an airport worker in a DayGlo vest directing everyone who had stopped. People were climbing out of their cars and taxis. Business men and women with briefcases and overnight bags confidently strode past. Mothers corralled small children while fathers unloaded bulky suitcases from trunks. It was chaotic. My plan to distract Pepperton was working. I pulled him towards the door.

"Where do you think you're going?" he asked, with a hint of panic in his whiny voice.

"We're almost there. Come on," I insisted.

Without waiting for a response, I tugged him towards the door again. The airport worker was making his way towards us.

"You can't park that here!" The worker shouted, jogging in our direction.

"I'm, uh, just showing my wife which way to go. I'll be right back," Pepperton yelled and then shoved me through the automatic doors before the airport worker got too close.

We paused to let a large group of bustling travelers pass in front of us then Pepperton dragged me over to a small alcove ringed with padded chairs.

"What do you think you're playing at, bringing me here?" he snarled.

"You said you wanted the disk. This is where it is," I said and tried to pull my arm out of his vice-like grip.

"Why would it be here?" His question held notes of disbelief.

"Henry told me to hide it here. And now I know why." I jutted my chin towards the gun he held down near his hip.

Pepperton yanked at the collar of my jacket, trying to peel it off me. It took some doing. My hair got caught in one of the buttons and I gave a sharp yelp as he thoughtlessly jerked it free. I rubbed my scalp where the small clump had once been. He draped my coat over his gun hand and gave a satisfied nod. Then he retrieved my cell phone from his own pocket. He noticed my confused look but didn't explain as he dialed a number and waited a few seconds.

"Yeah, just about. I need you to come help me." He paused. "Look, we don't have time to argue. We're real close to getting our hands on this thing. Come meet me. I'm at Logan. Departures, Terminal A."

He hung up and gave me his half-grin, which highlighted the crazy in his eyes. "You think you're so clever. Let me guess, the disk is somewhere past security." He wasn't really asking, so I didn't answer. "Even if I don't have a gun I can still kill you. You know that right?"

The look in his eyes made my heart forget its rhythm. I swallowed hard and glanced around for inspiration on what to do next. Nothing came to me.

"We're going to wait here until my friend joins us. Then we'll go. He'll go first to make sure you don't run off before I get through," Pepperton explained. "Let's go park the car while we wait."

He guided me back to the doors of the terminal. I wanted nothing more than to wipe the smug look off his face, but we both knew he was winning. I had hoped to lose him just past security. But if there were two of them, I knew it would be impossible.

Pepperton's cursing brought me out of my frantic, internal attempts to plan my escape. I looked up just in time to see a tow truck trundle past with the old, grey Buick hooked up behind it. I let out a laugh before I could catch myself.

Following a sharp blow to the side of my head, the next thing I knew I was down on the sidewalk. I looked up into Pepperton's cold, dark eyes.

"Oh dear, you tripped again. You really ought to be more careful, honey," he said in a loud voice for the benefit of the passersby.

He hauled me to my feet and shoved me once more through the automatic doors, into the airport. After a quick survey of the area, he found a secluded spot and marched me over to it.

"We'll just have to wait here until my associate arrives," he hissed.

He shoved me down onto one of the metal, cushioned chairs and plopped down next to me. We sat in silence for twenty minutes. I tried catching the eyes of anyone who came by, but they were all in too big a hurry to pay us any attention. Panic rose inside of me. I couldn't see a way out of this.

"I have to use the restroom," I tried.

"You can go once I have the disk," he muttered.

It was my last idea. My heart sank. It was over. I had no more plays to try. The only thing left to do was to get past security so Pepperton would have to ditch his gun. Then maybe I'd be able to make a break for it. Pepperton bolted up from his chair causing me to do likewise. I followed his gaze to a man walking towards us with his head down. My heart leapt into my throat when I saw the second man flash what appeared to be a police badge. Pepperton noticed my hopeful glance. But instead of looking worried, he laughed and nudged the new guy.

"Sorry to get your hopes up princess, but it's not real." Pepperton tapped the fake badge. "This is so we can forcibly restrain you once we get past security, if you try to get away. You tell anyone that we're holding you against your will, we flash that and tell them we're transporting a prisoner. They won't bat an eye. So don't even *think* about doing anything stupid."

I wanted to weep. The ache of desperation was starting to consume me. Pepperton turned his back slightly to talk to his partner. I decided it was now or never. While they were conversing, I tried to slip out of my seat, slowly and without making a sound. But no sooner did I try then I caught my foot on the leg of the chair and toppled over. Pepperton and bad guy number two crowded around to scoop me up off the floor.

"Do that again, and I pull the trigger," Pepperton said, pinching my bicep in his deceptively strong fingers.

I stopped fighting and let the strength in my legs give way. Pepperton wasn't having it. He shoved the jacket-gun into my back and growled at me to stand. I thought my heart was going to burst from my chest as we got closer and closer to the security checkpoint. I tried to look around for someone – anyone – who could help me, but Pepperton loomed behind me and shoved me forward. All I could hear was the blood rushing in my ears. *This is what it feels like to know you're about to die,* I thought.

My vision tunneled until all I could see was the metal detector getting closer and closer. I watched as Pepperton's partner made his way through the line about fifteen people ahead of us. He joked and smiled easily with the security guard while his ticket and ID were checked. The last ounce of hope flared inside me. I didn't have my ID! They wouldn't let me through without it.

As if reading my mind once more, Pepperton whispered,

"Don't worry, I grabbed your wallet when I grabbed your phone."

The rollercoaster plunged me down the last and final drop. I closed my eyes and felt him slip my wallet into my pants pocket. I let Pepperton guide me, shuffle step, shuffle step, like a lamb to the slaughter. I felt a tear slip down my cheek as we got closer to the metal detector. Five people away, shuffle step. Four people away, shuffle step. Three people away, shuffle –

"Kaly?" A voice I recognized but couldn't place called to me through my gloom.

Pepperton and I whipped around simultaneously. I did a double take. I had to rub my eyes to make sure I was really seeing what I thought I was seeing. Standing there like a superhero, surrounded by a gleaming backlight of glory, was Detective Dwyer and his partner Stanton!

I wanted to kiss them both repeatedly. I have never been happier to see anyone in my life. I felt like I could breathe again. Like I had been held under water for a long, long time, and I was finally breaking the surface. I savored the deep, sweet breaths. Color returned to my black-and-white world. The look on Pepperton's face was priceless.

"What? How? That's not...." Pepperton stuttered.

"Barlow Pepperton, I presume?" Detective Dwyer said, sizing Pepperton up from head to foot. The detective's appraisal lingered on my coat, still wrapped around Pepperton's hand. "I'm going to need you to put that coat down, Mr. Pepperton." Dwyer's voice was calm and low.

Pepperton gripped my arm so hard I knew it would leave

marks. He swiveled his head in every direction, weighing his options. Finally, he sighed and slowly relaxed his clenched fingers. I rubbed the angry, red blotches he left behind. Then without warning, he gave me a swift shove into Dwyer's outstretched arms and took off in the opposite direction.

"Go after him!" Dwyer yelled to his partner.

Stanton was already on the move. Dwyer and I had to disentangle ourselves before we could get to our feet. I wish I could blame our fall on my momentum, but Pepperton hadn't pushed me that hard.

"He has a partner," I exclaimed and pointed out the man who was watching us with eyes wide and mouth hanging agape.

It was as though he was frozen where he stood, just past the full-body scanners. My pointing brought him out of his daze, and he turned to make a break for it.

"Boston PD, stop that man!" Dwyer shouted, alerting the TSA agents to the fleeing hoodlum.

The security agents sprang into action and tackled him a few yards beyond the first gate. Dwyer started to move in their direction but then stopped and turned to me. "It was just the two of them?"

I nodded. "How did you know where I was?"

"Your friend Becca called me. She saw Pepperton force you into his car. She took down the license plate and called the precinct looking for me," he explained.

People gawked as they circumvented us to get to the security checkpoint.

"We put an APB out on the plates and got a response

from airport security when they towed the vehicle. The guy outside directing traffic told me where you came in. You're lucky you didn't get any farther, or I might not have found you in time."

I gave a humorless laugh as I ran a hand through my hair.

"You need to come to the precinct so you can fill me in on what in the name of Peter, Paul, and Mary is going on. But first I need to go make sure my partner's all right. Can I trust you to come on your own?" He lifted an eyebrow at me.

"Where am I gonna go?" I said, trying to be funny.

He wasn't amused, so I just nodded.

"Bring him out front and wait for me," he instructed the TSA agents who were holding Pepperton's partner.

Dwyer showed them his badge, and they nodded. Then the detective took off in the direction his partner had taken.

"Kaly!" Becca shouted from across the crowded atrium.

"Becca?"

My uncertainty only lasted a minute before I was running towards her, grateful to see my best friend when I needed her most. Becca bent down to grab something, but the crowd was too dense for me to see what it was. I could tell by the way she was moving that it was heavy, whatever it was.

When I finally reached her, I realized it wasn't one thing, it was two. With her left hand she was pulling a large rolling suitcase. In her right hand was a dog crate, big enough to hold an English bulldog.

I gasped when I caught site of the crate. I slid to my knees in front of its door just to see for myself that it was who I thought it would be. Mort gave a soft whimper when I came into view. I couldn't help myself, I hugged him, crate and all, ignoring the looks of those around me.

"He's okay?" I smiled at Becca.

"Yeah, but your closet door isn't. Mort nearly tore a hole through it trying to get out."

I felt the tears coming before they ever blurred my vision.

"Kaly, what is going on?" Becca demanded.

I looked at Mort, then over at the suitcase, and then back up to her. "I don't understand. Why did you bring all this?" I asked.

"You tell me!" she nearly shouted.

I sat on the floor with Mort for a moment. My brain trying to make sense of things. "How would I know why you brought this stuff?" I said with exasperation.

"Henry said you could explain."

"Henry? You spoke with Henry?!" I squeaked.

"Outside your apartment. Just after I saw that guy force you into his car. I tried to get to you, but I was too far away. All I could get was the license plate number. I'm sorry, I tried to reach you." Becca's voice broke, and she crumpled to the floor next to me, tears pouring down her face.

"It's okay, you saved me, Becca. You saved me. Your call to Detective Dwyer, your information on the license plate. That's how he found me in time. It's okay, Becca, it's okay." I hugged her, and we sat rocking back and forth on the floor.

People stared as they skirted around our small circle of floor space in the middle of the airport. We both had to let the sobbing run its course before we were able to talk again.

"Henry said he would find you. He told me to pack what I could, pick up Mort, and come here. He said we had to get out of town and that you would explain why once he found you. What's going on, Kaly? Why do we have to leave? Are we in danger?" Becca finally managed to get it all out around her hiccups.

"It's a long story, Becks. Did he say where you should go once you got here?" I asked, pushing myself up off the floor.

"He said to go to... to where the private planes take off. I don't... I don't know where that is exactly," Becca replied in a shaky voice.

"It's a ways from here. I think we'd better get a taxi. Come on," I said, lugging Mort's crate off the ground. "I'll explain on the way."

I felt a brief pang of guilt about my promise to Detective Dwyer, but then I remembered waking up to Pepperton's hand over my mouth and I didn't give it another thought. I just had to get away from all of this, and I needed to see Henry again. I knew I would be safe if I could just get to him.

It took a while to find a taxi that would agree to transport Mort. By the time we pulled up to the private terminal just north of the main airport, I had managed to explain what I could to Becca.

"You expect me to believe this is all about aliens?" Her voice was flat.

"I know it sounds crazy, but look at what's happened lately? None of this has been anywhere close to normal." I whispered, making sure the cabbie didn't overhear me.

It took a few minutes to wrestle Mort's crate back out of the taxi. We gave our names at the desk of the only gate that was open, and the perky girl behind the counter informed us that our plane was waiting for us on the tarmac. She gave us some instructions and we were on our way.

I don't think I'd ever gotten through security so quickly. Next thing I knew we were standing outside once more, staring at a small Lear jet. It sat like a gleaming beacon of safety and freedom, waiting with a metal staircase leading up to the open, inviting door.

Becca stopped abruptly. "He said we probably won't be able to come back."

I looked at her and then at the plane. I could hear sirens from somewhere not far off. A feeling of dread took root in my stomach. I thought about my clinic and my apartment. Then I thought about the break-ins and the gunfight in the alleyway. I thought about the life I had built here, but then I thought about being followed and kidnapped. Indecision held me rooted to the spot. Uncertainty plagued me as I considered my choices.

But then, Mort gave a happy bark from inside his crate. He wiggled so much I had to set him down to keep from dropping him. I glanced at the plane, and there, standing in the doorway, was Henry. He smiled and waved when he saw us. That's all it took. I had made my decision.

"I don't feel safe here anymore. If we stay, they won't stop coming after us. I'm going, but you have to make the choice for yourself," I told Becca.

She looked at me for a moment and then rolled her eyes. "There'd better be a smokin' hot guy for me too wherever we're going."

I laughed and was about to grab Mort's crate when a baggage handler walked up and offered to carry our cases. I made a "by all means" gesture, and Becca and I walked towards the plane and our new lives.

Epilogue

I'd like to tell you it was like a scene out of the movies. That I romantically boarded the plane and flew off regally into the sunset with the man of my dreams. But this is me we're talking about here.

Henry bounded down the steps to greet us, and just before I reached him, I felt my toe catch an invisible crack in the pavement. I fell spastically into Henry's arms, watching in horror at the surprised look on his face. But then he said two words that were even better than, "and they lived happily ever after," to an accident-prone girl like me at least.

With a twinkle in his eye and a mischievous grin on his perfect lips, he looked at me and said those two magic words that won this maladroit's heart.

"Not again."

ABOUT THE AUTHOR

Kara Piazza is also the author of the soon-to-be-released, exhilarating novel *The Seeker Initiative*. *Seeker Initiative* is Kara's first young adult, full-length novel, and it will be the first book in the series she has planned for her protagonists. Kara is also currently working on a follow up novel to *The Maladroit* along with an anthology that will give backstory to some of the "characters" you will read about in the sequel to *The Maladroit*. She also authors The Writing Piazza Blog, where she documents her journey through the harrowing process of writing and publishing her novel series. Kara currently lives in Arizona with her amazing twin boys, their pug Neptune, and their gigantic cat Boots.

You can connect with Kara through her website www.thewritingpiazza.com/blog/ or through social media.

Facebook: www.facebook.com/thewritingpiazza
Twitter: @writingpiazza
Instagram: @thewritingpiazza